TUMULT BEHIND THE TUBE

In the glamorous, glass-towered headquarters of a giant television network, talent and drive are no substitute for ruthlessness—or a good body. But back-stabbing becomes a grisly reality when the much bally-hooed series "Harbor Heights" dies in the ratings and a body turns up with a switchblade poised gracelessly between the shoulders.

Enter Matt Cobb, a network troubleshooter who specializes in scandal, but whose calling card is detection. The killer's trail leads from a lavish Connecticut mansion, where the nubile daughter of a network executive joins the hunt, to the pinnacle of power—a dizzying penthouse suite on New York's Sixth Avenue, where some people take the ratings seriously, dead seriously.

"A CLEVER, ENTERTAINING THRILLER . . . eminently readable, and the television business provides a new and interesting milieu." *Library Journal*

"A TOUCH OF THE GOOD, OLD-TIME PRIVATE EYE YARN . . . keeps the reader engrossed."

Pittsburgh Press

Killed in the Ratings

WILLIAM L. DeANDREA

 AVON
PUBLISHERS OF BARD, CAMELOT AND DISCUS BOOKS

Though similar systems have been discussed as possibilities for the future, the ARGUS system of audience measurement does not exist. It was created to meet the needs of the story. The same is true of all people, incidents, and institutions. Any resemblance to any actual person, incident, or institution is strictly coincidental.

AVON BOOKS
a division of
The Hearst Corporation
959 Eighth Avenue
New York, New York 10019
Copyright © 1978 by William DeAndrea
Copyright © 1978 by Harcourt Brace Jovanovich, Inc.
Published by arrangement with Harcourt Brace Jovanovich, Inc,
Library of Congress Catalog Card Number: 77-85185
ISBN: 0-380-43612-4

First Avon Printing, April, 1979

AVON TRADEMARK REG. U.S. PAT. OFF. AND IN
OTHER COUNTRIES, MARCA REGISTRADA,
HECHO EN U.S.A.

Printed in the U.S.A.

For my mother and father

Sometimes people call it the Tower of Babble.

It erupts from Sixth Avenue the way the igneous rock it's made of once erupted from some prehistoric volcano. Thirty-seven stories of somber stone and nonreflecting brown glass, it stands in eye-catching contrast to the gleaming spikes of the other skyscrapers; negative space in a sculpture of mirrors.

Its official name is Network International Headquarters, shortened in telegrams and interoffice memos to NetHQ. Architecturally, NetHQ is unique, but functionally, it is one of four. Evenly spaced along Sixth Avenue (only tourists and letterheads say "Avenue of the Americas"), these four office buildings are the focus of the process that determines what 200 million Americans will be offered during the six-hours-plus per day the average television set is turned on.

From the outside, there's nothing about NetHQ that marks it as the nerve center of a TV and radio network and the corporate octopus it spawned to support it, with the exception of the tasteful sign in the plaza, proudly but quietly proclaiming the world-famous nonverbal symbol that identifies the Network instantly.

But, from the minute you step inside, you know it's different. You can *feel* it. *I* did, for maybe the thousandth time that May morning as soon as the brown-glass and bronze revolving door spun me out into the marble lobby. Does Exxon, for example, line people up in *their* lobby to sell tickets for a tour of the corporate headquarters?

Six years ago, after I'd just been hired by the Network, I took the tour, feeling just like a kid on Christmas morning. Now I'd gotten used to the toy, but not tired of it, and I envied the school kids anxiously waiting for the teacher to dole out the tickets, because they had the thrill of seeing all the hardware ahead of them for the first time.

They'd see the bottom two-thirds of the building. The bottom third would kind of ease them into it; it contains the departments whose business it is to deal directly with the public (Ticket Services, Audience Relations, exhibits, restaurant), and the local TV and radio stations.

The middle section of the Tower is the real science-fiction part, the nuts-and-bolts section, a honeycomb of studios and control rooms; Network News and Network Operations. Here is where the soap operas and game shows come from, and where the prime-time shows from the West Coast are sent out over Ma Bell's coaxial cables to stations all over the country, and from there to your house.

What the students *wouldn't* see was what went on in the top nine floors of NetHQ. Kids wouldn't be interested, anyway. It takes an adult's eyes to see that this is where it all *really* happens; that in these nine floors of pristine white offices decisions are made that affect the eating, sleeping, lovemaking, even the *bladder* habits of America.

And it's not only television the people who work in the offices are concerned with, either. There's radio, of course, but there's also records and tapes. Movie theaters. Industrial and consumer electronics. Books and magazines. And the Minneapolis Hoops of the NBA.

I once cherished dreams of being a Minneapolis Hoop, if I couldn't be a New York Knickerbocker, but I was only pretty good, and if you stop growing at six-two, you'd better be a whole hell of a lot better than pretty good if you want to play pro basketball. I wound up working for the Network.

I got on the computer-controlled, high-speed, stainless steel elevator that would whisk me to my office on the thirty-fifth floor. I had a kind of homesick feeling as the numbers of the production floors blinked when I sped by. I had to remind myself I had risen above all that.

At the Network, and I suppose in any large corporation, there is no standing still. If you are not moving up, you are *backing* up. If you turn down a promotion, you sign your career's death warrant. Being happy with what you've got is the one sin that is never forgiven.

Until just a little over three years ago, I had been rising slowly but perceptibly through the ranks of the news department of the local TV station. I'd been hired as a desk assistant, and had made it up to associate producer, the same job Mary Tyler Moore is supposed to have had. It's a lot tougher and a lot more exciting in real life, and I loved it. I looked forward to the day I might even become a full-fledged producer.

Then, I got my Big Break. One afternoon, word filtered down from on high that I was to report to the office of Mr. Hewlen, the Lord and Master of the Network. He was a legend in the industry. Mr. Hewlen had visualized his empire back in the days when you needed headphones to hear a radio program.

Mr. Hewlen, at that time, was still President as well as Chairman of the Board. At eighty, he was still running the day-to-day operation of the Network, practically single-handed. Even today, he still made all the Major Decisions.

The fact that I, Matthew Cobb, should be a Major Decision was a shock in itself. I covered up my nervousness before I walked across that enormous penthouse office to come face to face with the tidy little man with the unruly shock of grey hair.

"Kid," he said (he always called me kid), "I've been looking over your record, and I've decided you're qualified, uniquely qualified, you might say, to fill an executive opening we've got. What do you say?"

What did I say, he asked. I was so thrilled, it took an effort of will to keep from vaulting his desk and hugging him. "Thank you very much, sir," I told him. "I'm honored."

He gave me the con man's grin, the one that means he's got you. "Good. Starting Monday, you're the new assistant to McFeeley down in Special Projects."

I thanked him again. I could *not* believe my luck. Unfortunately, I had been a little confused. I had thought he meant Special Events, which at our Network means space shots, and coronations and things like that. It's a common mistake. It didn't take me long to find out why.

The Network doesn't talk about the Department of Special Projects. Special Projects is the guerrilla band of Broadcasting. We wait in the weeds until some incident pops up that could harm or embarrass the Network. For example, if an important congressman has a favorite show, we'll find out what it is and whisper to the programming department not to cancel it until *after* the licensing bill is dealt with. We'll follow the kleptomaniac star around and pay for what she stole. We do everything that's too touchy for Public Relations, and too messy for the legal department.

Once I knew what I'd be doing, it was easy to see what my "unique qualifications" for the job were: I was at home on the street, but I could fake it well in society because I had mingled with the children of the Beautiful People at the small, snooty upstate college that gave me its one basketball scholarship that year. I had investigative experience, having been an MP after the NBA didn't draft me but the Army did. And I had contacts in both the press corps *and* (probably most important) the New York Police Department. And I wasn't indispensable anywhere else in the Network.

The three years since I had joined Special Projects had been interesting, to say the least. Sometimes, it had also been a little sickening, but I'd been in the same place for three years, and at the Network, if you're not moving up, you are backing up.

Then, the week before, I had gotten what was maybe my second Big Break. Hugh McFeeley, my boss, had gone into the hospital to have a hip joint replaced, and for six months, at least, Special Projects was mine. Maybe I could do something spectacular enough to get promoted out of it, and into Programming or Production; something more like communication and less like manipulation.

The elevator whooshed to a stop. The door slid open, and a cheery little bell announced my arrival. I waited a second for my internal organs to snap back to their proper places, then stepped out onto the thirty-fifth floor. You can tell how important you are to the corporation by how high up you are in the building. Special Projects has a tiny corner on the floor with the Programming Department. Only the President and the Sales Department, on the thirty-sixth, and Mr. Hewlen in the penthouse are above us.

The sterile aspirin white of the corridor is softened at that time in the morning (about nine) by splashes of color from the stenographic pool. Every year, the Network broadcasts five beauty contests, but I've yet to see a beauty queen we couldn't beat with someone from our own tower. And they never seem to get any older. Personnel must harvest a new crop of beautiful girls every six months.

It was nine oh one and sixteen seconds when I walked into the outer office, but nobody expects the boss to be on time, anyway. Jasmyn Santiago, the secretary I'd inherited while McFeeley was out, smiled me a Cuban sunrise and said, "Good morning, Mr. Cobb."

"Good morning, Jazz. Anything pressing?"

She'd been doing her nails. She blew on them to dry them. She was brown and bright and bouncy, and so cute not even blue nail polish and white lipstick could ruin her.

"Yes, sir, there's a few things." She picked up the report from the graveyard shift people. I was glad I didn't have to rotate into *that* duty anymore.

"Kenny Lewis is in trouble again," she said, "possession of cocaine up in Connecticut."

"Okay," I said. "We'll let him sit there for a day or so before we see about springing him." Kenny Lewis is a juvenile delinquent Special Projects has to get out of hot water about once a month. We do it to keep his mother happy. You would be shocked to find out who his mother is, and so would he, but she is a woman the Network wants kept happy. I think she'd do better by her secret son if she just left him alone, but mine not to reason why, mine but to take orders.

"What else?" I asked Jazz.

"News wants coffee and doughnuts on election night this year. They say pizza gives them a heartburn."

"The Anchorman's just getting old." I grinned.

Jazz was shocked. She thinks the Most Trusted Man in America could stroll across the Hudson any time he took a notion to.

"Okay, who's here? Shirley? Put her on it, when she gets a chance." Shirley Arnstein wasn't exactly one of the Network sexpots, but I wouldn't have traded her for ten of them. She came to us out of Washington, where she had been on the staff of a certain congressman who had been caught satisfying his private urges with the public's money. Shirley hadn't been the fringe benefit, she'd been the one who had actually done the work. Until the scandal broke, she had, in effect, been a United States congresswoman. She was plain-looking, and came across as shy, except when representing the Network. She once woke the mayor of Buffalo, New York, at three A.M. to chew him out for lack of cooperation on a missing persons case she was conducting up there for us. She was going semisteady with Harris Brophy, who was my top field agent, the way I had been McFeeley's.

11

Jazz consulted her list. "You got two phone calls, too, just before nine. One, no name, no message, will call back, and one from upstairs. Mr. Falzet wants to see you."

"Swell," I said drily. "You saved the best for last, huh?"

"Sure," she said smiling. She pronounced it "chure." It was the only trace of an accent she showed. "That way, you don't start swearing and I have to repeat everything."

"Well, don't let it happen again," I said.

"Yes, sir, Boss." She saluted. Two weeks ago, she'd been giving orders to *me*, or at least passing them on from McFeeley. She was probably the one indispensable person in the department.

I told her I'd be back in a little while, and went upstairs to see Thomas Falzet. He was President of the Network, the second one we'd had since Mr. Hewlen kicked himself upstairs half a year ago.

I presented myself to the receptionist, who told me to take a seat. I knew he had me cooling my heels for effect; he wasn't busy with anything, especially not at a quarter after nine. When you're the president of a corporation, they don't pay you hundreds of thousands of dollars a year to *work*, they pay you to be responsible for whatever happens. It's a good system. That way, they can fire *you* when things go wrong. Could you imagine General Motors canning the production line workers because profit was down?

While I was waiting, I sized up the receptionist, trying to decide if Falzet was sleeping with her. He had a reputation for stuff like that. She had the repressed bombshell kind of look, as though she were trying against the odds to look unsexy. I finally decided she was pure, because she looked too smart to try to look innocent if she was really guilty, so she must naturally look innocent. The old doublethink. The President called me in before I started the triplethink process on the poor girl.

Falzet didn't stand up when I came into the room, which would have been only polite. He really didn't care much for me.

"Sit down, Cobb," he said. It was an order more than an invitation. Falzet was in his late fifties, which is actually pretty old for a broadcast executive to be promoted to President. He looked younger, though. He had the horsy-faced good looks of a John Kennedy and only a touch of grey at the temples. I had seen him in action, and he was

12

a very smooth operator, but he saved it for the paying customers. With the hired help, he wielded the whip.

After I sat, he pretended to work some more, then looked at me and said, "I understand you've been doing some fieldwork for yourself, Cobb." There was still some Dixie in his voice.

I admitted it.

"Well, stop," he said. "It's against company policy for executives on the vice-presidential level to do that."

I'd figured it was coming. "Mr. Falzet, I'm only acting vice-president. I—"

"Cobb, the Network doesn't *utilize* manpower that way."

I majored in English in college. I would be an English teacher today if I hadn't been drafted, but I'm not pushy about it. I can turn perfect grammar on and off, mostly off because it sounds funny. But there are certain words and phrases that drive me up the wall, and Falzet habitually used every one of them. I heard "utilize" and winced. I also winced when he said I should go along with the "general consensus of opinion more off-tin."

"Something the matter with your eyes, Cobb?" he asked.

"No, sir." I made my face earnest. "Mr. Falzet, I appreciate the position of the Network, but right now, I *need* me. I'm sure you know Special Projects is the smallest department in the whole corporation. With McFeeley out, we're down to six, counting me. Brophy is working with the Russian embassy for that Olympics thing, Arnstein is woodshedding that actress who's up for the Virgin Mary spot in the Easter special. I need Santiago at the desk. The other two just came on. So, if anything else comes up that takes any experience, either I'll have to do it myself, or we'll have to fly somebody in from the Coast."

That did it. His statement to the stockholders had been a promise to economize. "Well, I can see where Special Projects is . . . ah . . . special. But don't go overboard, Cobb, understand?"

"Yes, sir, I'll be careful."

"Good. You do that, and we'll all stay out of trouble."

> *"Say the secret woid, the duck comes down,*
> *and you win a hundred dollars."*
> —Groucho Marx,
> "You Bet Your Life" (NBC)

I went back to my office to stay out of trouble. I busied myself with two great American pastimes: resenting the boss and watching TV. That was one of the really great things about filling in for McFeeley; as a vice-president, he rates a big color console in his office. That way, when a VP has nothing special to do, he can evaluate the product.

I grabbed a handful of purple jelly beans from the bag I kept locked in the desk, and settled back to watch "Agony of Love." If I see a soap opera, no matter how terrible, three days in a row, I'm hooked. I had actual withdrawal symptoms when "Dark Shadows" was canceled.

"Agony of Love" was getting good. Hank and Jessica were in the middle of an incredibly explicit (for TV) bed scene. They were sighing and moaning their heads off, and this was only Tuesday.

Just at the most suspenseful moment, when Jessica called Hank "Bill," the phone rang.

I lowered the volume and picked up the phone. "Yes, Jazz?"

"I have a caller on the line for you, Mr. Cobb."

"Who is it?"

"He won't say. He says he's the same person who called before."

The Network, as you would imagine, gets more than its share of crank calls, but they usually unload them on the switchboard girl. "What does he want to talk to me about, Jazz?"

"He *says* something personal and private. He told me to mention a Miss Monica Teobaldi."

That was the password, all right. "Put him on," I said.

"Mr. Cobb?" said a man's voice.

"Speaking."

14

"I've got to talk to you." The voice was a tenor, not squeaky, but under tight and precarious control.

"So talk away," I invited.

"No! In person. In private. But not in your office."

"Where then?" I hate games on the phone. "Times Square on New Year's Eve?"

"Dammit! I'm going right to the FBI with this. To hell with you *and* your Network!"

"Hold it. Don't hang up." I heard him grumble, but the line stayed open. "Where does Monica Teobaldi fit in with this?"

There was a moment's hesitation. "Nowhere. She's a friend of mine. She told me about you, said you were smart. Said you could be trusted."

"Yeah," I said, "I'm a prince. Can you see your way clear to giving me a little hint of what this is all about?"

"Why?"

"Why? Because there are eight million stories in the Naked City, and the best way to give yours an unhappy ending is to meet strangers with absolutely no idea of what you're doing it for. I want at *least* to know I'm going to be interested."

His control was going. "Damn you! Are you interested in your precious Network? The whole goddamn *industry?* Do you want to know the truth about Walter Schick?"

This fellow certainly had a flair for the right word. Monica was personal, but Walter Schick was business. Walter Schick was Mr. Hewlen's son-in-law. He was also Tom Falzet's predecessor as President. He'd served from November until this January, when he'd driven his Mercedes off an icy road near his Connecticut home. He'd been in a coma since, and anyone with a coin to flip could predict his future as well as the doctors could.

"I'm interested," I told the phone. "Where and when?"

"Hotel Cameron, eight tonight. Ask for Vincent. You know where that is?"

"Of course. I suggested Times Square right off, didn't I?"

"Stop making jokes!" The control was shot. "Just remember this: if I'm not there, find a guy named Vern Devlin, and ask *him* about it."

His receiver banged down. I replaced mine gently. I had to go see him. It seemed to me Vincent was intimating that Schick had been half murdered; that the accident that had wrecked his brain hadn't been an accident. And that the

15

Network, the whole *industry* was in trouble. What could that mean? CBS put out a contract on our executives?

Even if it *was* a pipe dream, if only a tiny percentage of what Vincent seemed to be saying was true, it had to be checked, and I had to be the one to do the checking, Falzet to the contrary. I knew I could trust me.

One good way to stop your imagination from running away with you is to find out if your facts are really facts. All I knew about my friend Vincent was that he'd learned to speak in Baltimore (from the way he'd said "jayooks") and that I was meeting him in a sleazy Times Square hotel that night.

The second one at least, was checkable. I got Jazz to put through a call to the Hotel Cameron to find out if a Mr. Vincent was registered. He wasn't, but they had a reservation for him, he'd be checking in sometime during the afternoon. So far so good.

I put a fistful of jelly beans in my pocket, and took the elevator down to my old haunts in Local TV News to look at the file on Walter Schick. It had a lot of information about how he'd gone from selling nylon stockings to selling commercial minutes, then rose step by step to the top of the Network, but nothing about his accident I didn't already know.

One thing I was pleased to see *wasn't* in the file was a story about his daughter Roxanne's running away with a smack dealer when she was fifteen. It was right after I'd joined Special Projects, and it turned out with the kind of happy ending nobody believes anymore. The pusher got twenty-five to life, Roxanne got straight, and I got a hefty raise for being the one who found her. And never a word leaked to embarrass her family *or* the Network.

It was a fat file. I read it through twice, trying to sneak up on the "truth" Vincent had in store for me. By the time I finished, it was quitting time.

I bucked the rush of nine-to-fivers sprinting for the exits, went upstairs, and picked up my briefcase. I left the Tower and took the bus home.

"Home" for now was an apartment on Central Park West that I couldn't possible have afforded until *I* was President of the Network. I was apartment-sitting for Rick and Jane Sloan, a couple of college friends of mine of vast and independent means, which freed them from some of life's more boring trivialities, like work. They had financed an archaeological expedition to Thailand, then decided it would be some bit of great fun to go along. What's two years, right?

Everybody has his own idea of fun. I had been stationed for a while in Thailand, during the middle part of the Vietnam fiasco, and Indochina is not a place I associate with fun.

I was also dog-sitting. Spot started yipping the instant I put the key in the lock. Spot had his points, but he was a sycophant. Nobody could possibly be as happy to see me as that dog pretended to be. When I walked in, he leaped in the air, wagging his tail furiously and licking my face on the fly.

"Yes, Spot," I said, "I'm delighted to see you, too." With one hand, I scratched him behind the ear, while with the other, I picked some dog hairs from my vest.

Spot was a Samoyed, a breed of medium-sized Siberian sled dog with pointy ears, a perpetually smiling face, and a cloud of pure white fur. His name is a joke. When Rick first showed me the puppy and told me his name was Spot, I said, "What spot?" and he said, "What's the matter with you, can't you see that gigantic white spot? Good God, Matt, it covers his entire body!" Rich people can get away with things.

I filled up Spot's water dish, put a TV dinner in the oven, then went for a quick shower and change. It was six-thirty when I finished eating, just enough time to walk the dog.

It was a warm night in late June, but a friendly breeze had blown the pollution away and the air was clear and comfortable. Spot and I headed into the park. He ran around, sniffing rocks and trees for a site he approved of. He finally picked a boulder on which a brilliant satirist or an idiotic bigot had spray-painted "WHITE SUPREMICY." It almost made me ashamed to be a Caucasian.

Out-of-towners think Central Park at night is a no-man's land with a mugger behind every bush. Totally untrue. At most, it's only every fourth or fifth bush. In any case, we escaped without injury. I returned to the apartment, grabbed a handful of change from the lap of an ivory Buddha by the door, transferred my jelly beans to my new suit, locked Spot inside, and headed downtown.

The Hotel Cameron was a five-story place just off Times Square, maybe a little less seedy than most of the others in the area, but still a hooker's haven. I passed one in the doorway, a redhead in a magenta dress. She gave me the big phony smile, but when I gave her a little one and a shake of the head, she shrugged to show no hard feelings. For her, the workday wasn't half over yet.

The desk clerk was a big fat guy with a tiny bald head. He looked as though he had started dieting, and was reducing from the top down. I could see him in a year's time with arms and legs like Popeye the Sailor. He was reading, of all things, *Forbes* magazine.

"What's good on the market?" I asked.

He looked up from his reading, smiling. "I can dream, can't I? No, look, they've got these funny little sayings in the back. Wait." He shuffled a few pages. "Here's one. 'Money is the root of all evil,'" he quoted, "'but that's one evil I'm rooting for.' Amen, huh?"

"Amen," I said.

"Looking for a room?"

"Looking for a friend of mine," I told him. "Is Mr. Vincent here?"

He checked the register. "I just come on, you know," he explained. "Vincent, Vincent. Ah, here we go, Charles Vincent, room 414. You ain't a cop, are you?"

"No. Do I look like one?"

"They never do, no more," he said mournfully.

I gave him my sympathy, and headed for the elevator.

"Sorry, pal," he said sincerely, "elevator's busted. Stairs to your left."

I made a face as I started up the stairs, thinking that if what Vincent wanted to tell me about was anything less than a plot to napalm Sesame Street, I would personally kick him in his head.

The stairs were carpeted in a neutral grey-beige, a color the management had picked, no doubt, to blend in with dirt. It was a good thing I was in shape, or the climb and the dust storm I kicked up would have made it impossible to breathe instead of only difficult. I was only puffing a little when I emerged on the fourth floor. The even numbers were across the hall and to my right, so I pointed myself in the right direction and walked to room 414.

There was no answer to my knock, but the door hadn't been locked, or even latched properly. My knuckles caused the door to creak open about thirty-five degrees. A black rectangle was all I could see of the room.

On the off chance he might have been taking a nap and had foolishly left the door open, I said, "Mr. Vincent?" and walked in.

I felt for a light switch to the right of the doorway. An overhead light went on, brighter than I expected. I blinked against it for a fraction of a second. When I opened my eyes, I saw the body on the floor.

My brain hadn't gotten much further along than being able to say, "Yep, that's a body on the floor, all right," when something hit me on the skull, hard. My brain went bright and hot, like a charge of napalm, then dark, like ashes.

The next coherent thought I had was *Wake up and answer the phone, idiot!* I didn't know how long it had been ringing, but the sound cut through my slowly returning consciousness, and got me moving again.

It's a conditioned response I share with a lot a people: *The phone must be answered.* It's a kind of degrading to have a Pavlovian reaction to the ringing of a bell, but I've never been able to kick it. I once lost a lady friend over something I interrupted to answer the phone.

I stood up and saw little flashbulbs go off in front of my face. I grabbed the door and held on. It had been eight o'clock on the dot when I knocked on the door; my watch read just past ten after now, so it hadn't been a long nap. My vision cleared, and I made for the phone, which was on a table by the window, stepping over the body on the way. It was the act of stepping over the body that made me aware again of exactly what was going on.

I turned around and took another look at the body. He was lying in a funny position that made him look more like a pile of two-by-fours than a person. He was wearing grey pants, black shoes and socks, and a red-and-white shirt. The red was caused by blood that oozed out around the imitation-pearl-handled switchblade someone had stuck in the middle of his back.

His face was kind of odd, because it wore a mild expression. It was a look of distaste, as though he had found a hair in his milk. He was about my age, had straight brown hair. His build was on the small side of medium. Women had probably called him handsome.

The phone was still ringing. I turned away from the body and answered it.

"Long distance. I have a person-to-person call for a Mr. Charles Vincent."

"Who's calling, please, Operator?"

A gruff voice down the line said, "Vernon Devlin."

"A Mr. Vernon Devlin," the operator echoed.

Well, Vincent, I found him for you, I thought.

"Mr. Vincent isn't feeling well, Operator," I said. "He isn't able to come to the phone." I'm a master of understatement.

"I'll talk to him," Devlin said. The operator thanked him and got off the line. "What do you mean, not well?" he demanded. "Is he hurt? Who is this, the police?"

"No, but it will be pretty soon. Who are you? A friend of Vincent's?"

"Yeah, we work together. Who are *you?*"

"My name is Cobb. Your friend wanted to meet me and tell me something. He said if anything went wrong to ask you about it. He's been murdered, what about it?"

"*Dead?*" he rasped. People do that all the time. You say, "The school burned down," and they say, "It caught *fire?*"

"Yes, dead," I assured him. "Stabbed. I just found him."

"Oh, God."

"Absolutely. Look, I want to call the cops, so I'll make this quick. I'm kind of a troubleshooter for a TV network, and Vincent had some for me to shoot. What do you know about it?"

"Oh, God," he said again. "Listen—Cobb is it? This is

20

big. This is very big. Don't call the cops. Get out of there, and forget about the whole thing."

"Forget it, pal. People saw me come up here. I'm calling the cops right now, good-bye."

Before I had the receiver an inch away from my ear, Devlin started yelling, "No, no! Wait!"

I put it back to my ear. "Now what?"

He sounded relieved. "Okay, I was off base with that suggestion. Call the cops, *but don't tell them anything!*"

"I don't *know* anything, putz!" I was getting irritated. Here I was in a cheap hotel room with a lump on my head and a rapidly cooling corpse on the floor, and this clown wants me to play games with the cops. "No way," I said.

"Well at least, don't mention me, okay? Look, I'm putting myself in your hands. My name is Vernon J. Devlin. I live in Fairfax, Virginia, and work in Washington, D.C., for Communications Research Incorporated."

"The ratings outfit?" *I* was doing it now. Everybody knows CRI is the independent research company that does the overnight TV ratings.

"Uh huh," he said. "Please, give me just one day on this. One day."

"Why should I?"

"Because I can tell you all about it. Look. This is Tuesday. I've got something important here Wednesday, but I can be in New York on Thursday. Please, give me a break on this. We can't talk about it on the *phone.*"

I let him sweat for a minute. "Okay," I said finally. "How do you plan to get here?"

"Train," he said. "I'll leave early in the morning and meet you at nine-thirty in Penn Station at the information booth."

"Right. Nine-thirty, Thursday. Wear a carnation."

"A what?"

"A carnation. A flower, in your lapel."

"Nobody does that anymore," he said. "I'll stick out like a sore thumb."

"Right you are. That's how I'm going to spot you."

"Oh, all right. You won't regret this, Cobb."

"You'd just better be there. Now can I call the ___"

"Police! Don't move!" There was a crack as the doorknob popped a hole in the plaster.

I didn't move. It's foolish to move when two guys with badges and guns tell you not to. These particular guys were mismatched; a young earnest kid straight out of "Adam-12," and a dumpy "Car 54" type.

"What took you so long?" I asked.

"Never mind that," Adam told me. "Put down that phone. Hold your hands against the wall."

I did. Car 54 gave his gun to Adam, them came over and kicked my feet back and apart, so if I took my hands away from the wall, I'd fall flat on my face. He frisked me expertly, then told me I could straighten up.

I turned around to see a plainclothesman entering the room. He was a wiry guy. He took off a grey fedora to reveal wiry grey hair. He told me his name was Detective Second Grade Horace A. Rivetz. I suppressed a suicidal impulse to ask him if he was as hard as nails when I told him my name.

The telephone was still lying on the table, off the hook. Rivetz brushed by me and picked it up. To my astonishment, he still had somebody to talk to. He asked a lot of questions, and said, "I see," sixteen times.

Finally he said, "Okay, Mr. Devlin. You going home now? Oh. Okay. Expect somebody from the Fairfax police tomorrow morning. Early. Let me have those phone numbers again. Thank you, Mr. Devlin."

He hung up the phone, regarding me dyspeptically. "Well, Mr. Cobb, Mr. Devlin tells me you discovered the body."

I admitted it.

"Well," he continued, "I got to clarify the legal situation here. You are not yet under arrest, but I'm detaining you as a witness, and on that basis, I'm gonna inform you of your constitutional rights." Rivetz had learned to speak in Flatbush. That dialect is supposed to be amusing, but it wasn't then. He didn't even have the good grace to be menacing, he was just bored. It was terrifying that a policeman should think finding me alone with a corpse was boring.

He gave me my rights from memory, not resorting to the Miranda card. I told him I had no desire for an attorney, and that I was giving up the right to remain silent, for now. I was going to tell him a lie, and I wanted to get it over with.

"What happened, Mr. Cobb? In your own words."

I've always loved that phrase. Who the hell else's words could I use? It didn't happen to anybody else.

I told Rivetz the whole story, with a couple of exceptions.

I edited the contents of Vincent's phone call to me, especially to omit the name of Walter Schick. There was no reason to keep Devlin out of it anymore, but I downplayed the intensity of his desire to be left out of the picture, and neglected to mention our little appointment for Thursday.

I told him I'd never met the deceased, but a mutual friend (Monica) had given him my name and told him to look me up when he was in New York, and that he had.

"He told me he wanted to talk to me about something, and that I should meet him here at eight. When I got here, I found him on the floor, somebody hit me in the head (see this lump?), and I was out for about ten or twelve minutes. The phone woke me up."

"When did you get here? At the hotel, I mean?"

"Couple of minutes before eight."

"Sure you didn't get here sooner? Didn't have time for a drink, a smoke?"

"Absolutely. Ask the desk clerk. I talked to him."

Rivetz assured me he would, but from the tone of his voice and the expression on his face, Spot would probably have to fix his own breakfast. I had to admit my story was pretty weak.

While I was talking with Rivetz, more detectives arrived, along with photographers and lab men. They had been buzzing quietly around the room the whole time. Just before the question about drinking and smoking, one had come over and whispered in his ear.

Rivetz stood up, saying, "Come with me, Cobb, I want the lieutenant to have a talk with you."

"Am I under arrest?" I asked, just wanting to know.

"Want to be?"

I went with him. He took me in an unmarked car to Homicide South, and had me wait on a worn-out bench in a room painted a leprous apple green, while he went in to talk to the lieutenant. There were plenty of policemen around to keep an eye on me, in case I got desperate and decided to make a break for it.

I waited a lot longer than I thought I would, which was probably the whole idea, before I was finally sent for. I was led into the lieutenant's office.

If anyone ever offers you a choice between luck and brains, take luck every time. I'd been calling on my brain, and it was doing nothing. Then luck greeted me in the form of Detective Lieutenant Cornelius U. Martin, Jr.

I was never so happy to see anyone in my life. I knew he was working Homicide, but I never figured he would get this case. There are too many lieutenants.

Even sitting down, he gave the impression of force, or maybe perseverance is a better word. He looked like a brown mountain, with curly white snow on top. He looked at me with his round, honest face, and said, "Matty, what have you gotten into now?"

Rivetz was incredulous. "You *know* this guy, Lieutenant?"

He not only knew me, he half raised me. Twenty-odd years ago, then-Patrolman Martin and his family moved in next door to us and busted our block. A lot of families moved away, but we couldn't afford to, so my folks gritted their teeth and made the best of it.

The best of it turned out to be pretty good. The Martins were the best proof of something a lot of folks, black and white, never get to learn: people are just people. The Martins are the best people around. You never saw two friendlier families than the Cobbs and the Martins.

The lieutenant's son, Cornelius U. Martin III, and I were inseparable as kids. You may remember us, we made a minor ripple in high school as the Corn-Cobb backcourt. Corny made All City, and of course you remember him in the NBA. He's coaching at a college in the Midwest now.

If it had been Lieutenant Martin in the first place, I might have handled it differently. I might have told him everything, and asked his advice, but damn it, now I was on the record with that lie, and I was stuck with it. When I told my story again for the lieutenant, I told it the same way.

When I was finished, the lieutenant said, "I don't believe you, Matty."

My voice has a tendency to crack at inopportune moments. "What?" I squeaked.

"I don't believe you. I don't believe you went to see a man in that dump just because he mentioned an old girl friend's name. Your mama didn't have any stupid children, Matty, and doing that would be very stupid."

I started to sputter a reply, but he cut me off.

"Hold it, Matty. I've got some reports coming in I've only just glanced at. Suppose you wait outside for about twenty minutes while I look them over." He looked me a warning. "Think about what the report might say, Matty."

Rivetz took me outside. My paranoia quotient hit a new high. What the hell was he talking about? Why me? This was going to take more than some purple jelly beans. I got Rivetz to accompany me to a vending machine, where I bought two Reese cups and a Pay Day.

"You got a sweet tooth?" Rivetz asked, as though a sweet tooth were a sure symptom of homicidal mania.

"No, I'm a diabetic bent on suicide."

"The time is coming," he promised, "when you ain't gonna think that's too funny." That was the end of conversation between us.

The lieutenant was very punctual. My watch made the elapsed time I'd been out of his office nineteen minutes and fifty-six seconds.

"Cigarette, Matty?" he offered as I sat down.

"You know I don't smoke, Mr. M.," I told him.

"That's right, I forgot." He lit one for himself, and blew a lungful in my direction. I couldn't tell if he was aiming for me or Rivetz, because the Flatbush Flash was on me like white on rice. I think he was afraid I was going to pull a tommy gun out of my nose and blast my way out.

25

Lieutenant Martin asked if they could take my finger-prints. "For comparative purposes, of course," he said. I knew he didn't have to ask, and he knew that I knew. I wondered what he was up to.

"Sure, go right ahead," I told him. I didn't have to go anywhere, an expert was sent for.

When he was finished, the questions began again.

"You were very good friends with the Teobaldi woman, weren't you, Cobb?" Rivetz included a leer with the question free of charge.

"Yes," I said.

"Did you go to bed with her?"

He was trying to get me ticked off, and doing an excellent job of it, too, but I was damned if I would let him see it.

"Occasionally," I said.

"When was the last time you saw her?"

"A little over two years ago."

"You haven't seen her since? Why not?"

"She got married."

"She's been divorced. She's been back in New York over six months."

"So I heard." I turned to the lieutenant. "What is he driving at?"

Lieutenant Martin looked grave. "According to Devlin, Charles Vincent wasn't the dead man's real name."

"So?"

"He says his real name was Vincent Carlson."

"Oh, Christ," I said.

"And Vincent Carlson was the ex-husband of Monica Teobaldi."

I always remember the next few moments as though they were a comic strip. *Gulp! Gasp! Choke!* Then I realized it would be hard to find a way to look guiltier, so I stopped goggling.

"Care to revise your story, Matty?" the lieutenant asked.

Should I? I decided not to. The news that the dead man used to be Monica's husband was bad news for Matt Cobb, but I couldn't see where it made any difference to the Net-work, and tying the Network into the mess wouldn't make the facts go away. I told them no thanks.

The lieutenant said in that case, I wouldn't mind signing a statement. I said I'd be delighted. A stenographer typed one up. I read it over and signed it, thereby adding perjury to all my other sins.

I was gambling with my future. The major portion of my job was to protect the Network. Whatever the connection between Walter Schick and the murder, I had committed myself to finding it and defusing it before it splattered all over the front pages. If I could pull it off, fine. If I blew it, I was through in the industry anyway, and jail is better than skid row. Cleaner, at least.

The lieutenant sent Rivetz out to check the movements of the dead man. Then he turned his big honest face on me, and my mind did a flashback to when he caught Corny and me in the cellar, giggling over a *Playboy* magazine. "I hope you know what you're doing, Matty," he said dolefully.

"Me too," I said.

"I know you didn't kill that man, Matty."

"Thanks. But is that Mr. M. or Lieutenant Martin speaking?"

"Both. Hell, I've known you since you were six years old. But there's evidence says you didn't do it."

I asked him what it was.

"You never mind. If it clears you, it might point to someone else. But your story is very, very cheesy, Matty. And Rivetz, well . . ."

He didn't finish, but I knew what he meant. Rivetz figured he'd walked into an easy collar. Homicide collars look good on the record. Rivetz hated the thought of it not being me. He wouldn't try to frame me, exactly. It's just that he'd view any evidence on the basis of whether it proved my guilt.

Lieutenant Martin shook a finger at me. "Just one thing, Matty. I'm your friend, but I'm still a cop. If you're lying to me, I'll put you in jail. You're too old and too big for me to go upside your head."

I had to smile.

"I'll do it," he said. "I wouldn't like to, but I will. It would be the same with Cornelius, too."

"Nah," I said. "You'd go upside his head, *then* put him in jail."

He laughed. It made me feel a lot better. "Go on, get out of here. Do you want me to get you a ride home?"

"No thanks. I assume you've had somebody talk to Monica Teobaldi."

"Yeah, she and her boyfriend went to the morgue with

27

one of my men and identified the body. And she confirms that story of yours, for what it's worth. You could have had it planned in advance."

"That would take a very devious person," I deadpanned.

"Yeah, well I know where to find one." He scratched his head. "You know, no matter what squad I'm on, sooner or later I get a case with *you* in it. It *looks* bad when you all the time have to investigate the neighbors' kid."

"Just the nature of our jobs, I guess."

"Then why don't you get another job, be an English teacher, like you were supposed to."

"Because I became addicted to money," I said. "I need it in larger and larger doses every week."

He laughed again.

I got serious. "You realize that I'm going to see Monica right after I leave here."

"I figured you would," he said quietly.

"Okay. I'm not skulking around about it. Tell the guy who's going to be tailing me, that if he loses me, that's where I'll be. Tell the guy who has Monica staked out, too."

He laughed. "You won't see a tail on you, Matty," he assured me. "But don't leave New York State, okay?"

"Sure." We shook hands, and I left.

The first thing I wanted was a telephone. There was a booth on the corner, but the vandal-proof phone had been ripped out and taken away. I could picture the triumphant inventor saying, "See? they couldn't vandalize it!"

The second booth ate my dime. A police doctor had told me the lump on my head was nothing serious, but it still hurt. As my irritation increased, it started to throb. I took a deep breath, held it, and walked on.

The next booth had one of those "tone first" phones, where you can find out if the phone works before you invest your money. Congress should pass a bill making them universally mandatory.

I dropped my dime, and put through a call to the local station owned and operated by the Network.

"Newsroom." The word was crisp and clear, and was said with just a touch of pardonable pride, just the way I used to say it.

"Jack Hansen, please." Jack Hansen was an award-winning crime reporter; an ex-cop, who had better sources than the Mississippi River. The only thing wrong with him was that he had too much journalistic integrity. Special

Projects had learned never to ask him to find out anything that would be embarrassing on the air.

"Jack Hansen."

"Jack, this is Matt Cobb."

"Oh, hi, Matt. What can I do you for?"

"Hi. Listen, have you heard about that murder in the Hotel Cameron tonight?"

"Yeah, I just got in with the film crew, we're cutting for the eleven o'clock news right now."

I looked at my watch. "Don't worry, you've got thirty-eight whole minutes. You do your best work under the gun, anyway.

"Jack, I need a favor. Dig a little deeper on this one. Check into this Vincent Carlson. Find out what the cops are thinking, and get back to me on it, okay?"

"Hmmm," he said. "Is there a story in it?"

"Could be," I admitted. "Of course, use whatever you dig up—"

"Goes without saying," he murmured.

"—but if you sit on it awhile, I may be able to give you a big—a huge story later on." I thought of something else. "Oh, by the way, Jack, who found the body?"

"Friend of the deceased. Cops haven't released the name."

God bless them, I thought.

"How soon do you want this, Matt?"

"As soon as possible. Call anytime, home or office. Don't let me hear it on the air first, okay?"

He said it was okay.

About a hundred yards after I left the phone booth, a vague uneasiness crossed the synapse in my brain and became an actual perception. Each of my footsteps had a quiet echo. I had a tail. He was easy to spot, once I knew he was there, by checking the nighttime reflections in car windshields.

I was angry and hurt at Lieutenant Martin, until I remembered what he had said: "You won't *see* a tail on you." He wasn't lying, he just underestimated my powers of observation. As it was, this guy was an unlikely candidate. He looked much too short to be a cop. Somebody should have told him about gumshoes. If his footsteps hadn't stopped each time I tried a phone, I never would have picked him up.

I decided to shake him, both to teach the lieutenant

29

not to play word games with an English major, and to give Shorty a few pointers.

I walked at an even pace up to a litter basket at the corner, and threw away a candy wrapper I had in my pocket. Then I turned the corner and ran like the proverbial bat out of hell. I let him hear my shoes echo on the pavement. I wanted him to be running, too.

About halfway down the block, I ducked into the vestibule of a small apartment building. I stood behind the glass and watched him run by. He ran all the way to the corner, looked both ways, and headed uptown. I waited a decent interval to give him a chance to get a good lead, then followed *his* path for a while, until I flagged a cab to take me to Monica's apartment.

*"Return with us now, to those thrilling days
of yesteryear . . ."*

—Fred Foy, "The Lone Ranger" (ABC)

The lobby of Monica's building had an intercom buzzer system, but I didn't want to use it. It was possible she didn't want to see me; either because she wasn't alone, or because she had a secret to keep.

I used a burglar's trick I had learned from Lieutenant Martin. I pushed a button at random, not Monica's. When the voice came on to ask what I wanted, I said, "It's about Joey."

Everybody knows someone named Joey, and the odds are pretty good that out of a given group of people, someone will care enough for their particular Joey to get curious. It took eight tries, until a lady in 11G said, "What about Joey?"

"It's about the bank," I said, "it's pretty complicated."

"Oh, Lord!" The door clicked as it unlocked.

It always works. No matter how friendly banks say they are in commercials, people still hate and fear them. "It's about Con Edison," is a good variation, for the same reason. I felt a little sorry for Joey when 11G started asking him questions.

It was a beautiful building, with hallways done up in blue and gold, and a plush carpet of royal blue on the floor. If they'd sunk less money into decor and spent more for security, they could keep undesirables like me out of there.

I hesitated for a second before pressing Monica's doorbell. I felt like one of those Mexican cliff divers looking down, trying to sort the water out from the rocks. I hit the doorbell. Chimes inside played the first four notes of "Nature Boy." Nothing. I waited fifteen seconds, then tried my fist.

"Come on, not again!" It was a loud groan in a man's voice, coming from inside. "Just a minute!"

A few seconds later, the door swung open and a muscular specimen with a red handlebar moustache said, "Honestly, can't you leave her alone? She *told* you people before she hasn't even seen her ex-husband since the summer."

He was barefoot and bare-chested, and wearing canary yellow pants in between. He couldn't have been as young as he looked, not and be dressed like that in Monica's apartment. I decided he was twenty-two.

"Sorry," I said officiously. "Routine." If he wanted to think I was a cop, I certainly wasn't going to disappoint him.

"Okay," he said, "come on in. Just remember, we were together all evening. All day."

I almost blew my own cover by recognizing aloud a print I'd given Monica a long time ago, a laughing clown. He didn't seem as happy as I remembered.

I sat on a sofa in the living room, leaving a wicker chair for my friend. It must have been a real treat on his bare back, but he had too much grace to mention it, especially to a cop.

A bedroom door opened partially, and Monica's head popped out. That beautiful tawny head. "I'll be with you in a minute, offic—Matt!"

Judging by her face, worrying about her wanting to see me had been a waste of time. "I'll be right with you. Talk to Tony for a minute."

Without a word, Tony got up to make drinks.

"Bourbon and Seven-Up," I said. I gave him a toothy grin. "Pleased to meet you, Tony."

He brought me my drink. "Same here," he said, reoccupying the wicker chair.

He had double-crossed me. He was being insidiously nice. I was dying to take out my doubts, fears, and frustrations on somebody (to say nothing of that clout on my head), and Tony was the right size and shape to make it interesting. He also had the air of the kind of macho freak that can be induced to take a swing without much trouble.

"Known Monica long?" I put it as offensively as I could.

It slid by him. He was sizing me up. Friendly, but closely. I let him take a good look.

"So you're Matt Cobb, huh?" he said at last.

I pleaded guilty.

"You're younger than I thought you'd be."

"So are you, if it comes to that. I'm the same age as Monica."

"Yeah, but she's got this big father-image conception of you, you know? So I thought you'd be older. She also says you're very handsome." His tone implied he didn't agree.

"How did my name happen to come up?" I asked.

"You'd be surprised at the number of things that can remind her of you, just in the studio at work. If the show was on your Network, that's probably all she'd talk about."

I told him I admired his broad-mindedness.

He tilted his head back and looked at me across his moustache. "Yup. It's a bummer, for sure. I'd never take it from another chick, but Monica is special. She's got something . . . she could be a Nazi—not that she would, of course—but even if she were, it wouldn't matter. I don't know what it is."

I did, but then I had known her longer. I knew the bad things, too. "Why tell me?" I asked him.

"Curiosity. To learn what keeps a chick—a *lady* like Monica hung up on a guy. And I *sure* want to know what could keep that guy away from her. You're not gay, are you?"

Mr. Tact. "No," I said wearily, "I'm hardly even cheerful." My belligerence was gone. Now I was only tired.

Tony was still serious. "I didn't think so. So what can it be? Why do you avoid her?"

"Some other time. It's too long and sad a story."

That was the instant Monica walked in, as though I'd given her entrance cue. She'd put on a hostess pajama in some clingy material with a softly colored floral print. She looked gorgeous.

She said, "Hello, Matt."

"We have to talk, Monica."

Tony said, "I, ah, better be running along," and went to the bedroom to get dressed. I sat looking at Monica.

You have seen Monica Teobaldi. She was an actress and a dancer, moderately successful and on the way up. Her career was made up of the things most moderately successful New York actresses' careers are made up of: Broadway, soaps, and commercials.

She was between shows on Broadway, but she had an

important role on another network's new soap, and of course all those commercials.

She was long and slim, but far from bony, and she moved with a dancer's kind of racehorse litheness and grace. Her face wasn't classically beautiful, but she had an innocent, round-eyed look that was irresistible. The eyes themselves were a pale, pale brown, almost yellow. Her hair was a color called old gold. Her breasts, small but perfect, asserted themselves against the flowered fabric.

Tony had dressed. He had a green shirt and a red jacket to go with the yellow pants. As unobtrusively as he could in an outfit like that, he walked to the door.

"Tony," Monica called, "thanks for everything."

He blushed. "It was my pleasure—I mean, I was glad to help."

Monica assured him she understood. He left us.

"What does he do," I asked Monica, "hire out as a test pattern?"

Her laugh was a bar from a Herbie Mann solo. "No, he's just joined the cast. Right out of college. He's remarkably talented, and very professional, so don't make fun of him, Matt, he's a nice boy."

"Boy," I said, "is the key word."

"Don't lecture me, Matt." A warning, friendly but definite. "This hasn't been an easy night. I had to identify the body. Tony has been a great help."

And a great consolation, I didn't say. "You seem to be taking it very well."

"What do you want me to do? Vince and I were through months ago. I tried to put him out of my mind, never see him again, and the next thing I know—"

There must have been something in my face she didn't like. I'm damned if I know what it was, but she got a look, and choked her sentence off. She studied her nails for a few seconds, punishing me by denying me her eyes.

Finally, she looked up and said, "It took a murder."

"What?"

"Vince had to be murdered before you would come and see me."

I didn't say anything, I was afraid to.

"I've been back in New York for six months now, Matt. You brushed me off on the phone, you don't answer my letters. That isn't like you."

"You hurt me, Monica."

"I didn't mean to."

"How in the name of God could you marry somebody without meaning to?"

That one had her stumped. She sat looking helpless.

There was no stopping me, now. I'd been saving it for two years. "All right. Carlson pleased you better than I did. Fine. I'm a big boy, I could handle that. But after what we'd been to each other, I figured I rated something more than a phone call after the fact."

She mumbled something.

"What?"

"I said I was afraid you'd talk me out of it." She stood up and started to pace. It was hard with Monica to tell where the actress left off and the person began.

She fixed me with her eyes. "You never needed me, Matt." It was an accusation. I started to deny it, but she cut me off, "You might think so, but it's not so. You were so so goddam *serene*. Anything I did was all right with you, even when I saw other men.

"Vince *really* needed me, me or somebody. And I loved him, too."

"So you divorced him," I said cruelly.

"Yes, I did," she whispered. "Vince just couldn't stop gambling. I tried to help him, I honestly did. It got to the point where I wasn't helping him, I was only destroying me. Then the threats started."

"Threats?"

She nodded. "Vince gambled his salary away, but he wouldn't touch mine. He once said he was still *that* much of a man, anyway. He borrowed money from loan sharks, and lost and kept losing."

"It's a disease," I said, inanely. It was as though her husband were dying of cancer and I tried to soothe her by telling her it was a disease.

"One day a phone call came," she said, ignoring the comment. "A man told me to ask my husband how many jobs an actress would get with acid scars on her face."

"So I left him. He didn't contest the action." She didn't try to defend herself, and I didn't judge her. It's easy to say we would have the guts to stick out a situation like that, but who really knows?

Monica's mistake was in not realizing you can't love people by changing them. They must change *themselves* for love of you, or you must adapt yourself to them.

35

"I was kidding myself when I thought I could be strong for Vince," she said. "I need someone to be strong for me. I *should* have called you sooner, Matt." She sat next to me on the couch and took my hand. "I think you would have saved me from a terrible mistake. I think we could still be good together, Matt."

"Same as before?" I asked.

"Same as before," she said.

I thought about it. Knowing Monica, I couldn't blame her for marrying Carlson; she was the kind of romantic who never could have resisted saving a man from himself, the way things happen in the movies. If anybody was to blame, it was the drama critic of the *New York Times*. If he hadn't raved over her performance, she wouldn't have been offered the gig with the Capitol Players, and never would have gone to Washington and met Carlson in the first place.

But loving Monica, I couldn't change her; and I couldn't twist myself into the shape of the kind of man I'd have to be to make her happy: the calm, strong father image Tony mentioned. Hell, I didn't even like being responsible for myself.

My head throbbed from thinking about it. "Do you have any aspirin?"

She took her hand away. Her voice was bitter with self-mockery. "Not tonight, dear, I have a headache."

"Not tonight, dear, a murderer caressed my skull with an ashtray."

Her look softened. "I'll see if I have any." She went into the bathroom. "Does it have to be aspirin?" she called.

"Anacin, Bufferin, anything," I answered.

"Midol?"

"It's my *head* that hurts, Monica," I reminded her. It struck us as terribly comical, and we laughed for a long time.

She was still laughing when she came back with two tablets and a cup of water. "I had some aspirin in my purse," she said when I looked at them suspiciously.

I shrugged, and swallowed them.

"What was Carlson going to tell me, Monica?"

"Didn't you tell the police it was something about a business deal?"

"I suggested it as a possibility, which they laughed off.

36

Come on, Monica, he said it was trouble, for the whole industry."

Her golden eyes widened. "Then you did lie to the police?"

"What was he going to tell me?"

"I backed up whatever you said, because I thought Vinnie misled *you!*"

"Goddammit, Monica, what was he going to tell me!"

"Don't yell at me. Anyway, I don't know."

"Monica, please. You *sent* him to me. He was *killed*. The cops know we were lovers, and some of them have a pretty strong notion *I* did it!"

The look on her face would have been the same if someone had hit her with a fist. "But . . . that's ridiculous!"

"Is it? Look at what *they* see. Dead husband, ex-wife's ex-boyfriend standing over the body. They think we both did it, you set him up and I killed him."

"But why?"

"Let them worry about that. By tomorrow, they'll have seventeen theories about our motive."

She took a deep breath, facing facts, but not liking them. "What should we do?" she asked.

"Answer some questions for me, all right?" She agreed. "Okay," I said. "First, why did Carlson call *me*, as opposed to an officer of the law, for example? He mentioned the FBI. How did he even know I existed in the first place? We never met."

"I told him about you. I was still seeing you when I first met Vince. I . . . I talked about you a lot."

"What did *he* say?"

"Not much, really. Nothing I can remember."

"And that's it? After two years, when he's in so much trouble he's killed for it, he remembers and comes to me?"

"No, Matt," she said. She took my hand again. "In August, I think," she began, then paused, to be sure, scraping upper teeth over lower lip. On her, it was beautiful.

"Late July, or early August, about a month after the divorce, I met him in a bar. He'd started having alcohol trouble along with the gambling trouble. He was very drunk. He started to cry when he saw me. He wanted to talk to me.

"I owed him that, at least. He told me he didn't want to do it—"

"Do what?"

She shook her head. "I asked him, but he just kept repeating it. He said he was doing it for me."

"Can you remember his exact words?"

Her face drew up in a pained expression, but she gave it a try.

"He said, 'I don't want to do it, but I've got to, you understand, don't you, Honeypot?' He used to call me Honeypot."

I said nothing.

She went on. "I asked him what he was talking about, and he said, 'I'm doing it for you, you know.' Then he said, 'The divorce doesn't make any difference to *them*,' or something like that. Then he told me not to worry.

"He told me he was the one who had to worry. I asked him what he had to worry about, but he wouldn't say. He just got very serious, the way drunks do, you know how they can be, and said, 'After I do this, Monica, I'll have nowhere to turn. *They'll* own me, all of them, and the industry will hate me, too.'

"Then he said, 'Honeypot, I hope this never happens to you, that you get in bad trouble with no one to turn to.' Then he said, 'Oh, I made a mistake, you'll always have your old boyfriend, Sir Galahad.' He made a remark about your collecting a fee in trade.

"I told him he was wrong, and I told him if he was that desperate, he should get in touch with you, that you could do things nobody else could. I wrote your name and phone number out for him."

I closed my eyes. "You used me, Monica. You used me as a club to beat that poor bastard over the head with. And he took you at your word. If he'd gone straight to the cops—" I cut myself off before I said, "he'd probably still be alive." Monica didn't need to hear that.

"But you *are* the best person to go to! I know you've helped lots of people. Hugh McFeeley once told me you were the one guy in the whole business straight enough to trust and smart enough to help both the Network *and* the poor slobs that get in its way."

Big help I was to Carlson, I thought.

She read my mind, or at least my face. "At least you went to see him. You tried. I'm really the guilty one."

"You? How? You gave him eighteen months out of your life."

"I mean later on, at that bar. I could have found out

what he was up to. He could *never* keep a secret, from me or anybody. He liked to talk about his problems, I could have found out and made him stop.

"But he embarrassed me. I couldn't get out of that bar fast enough. Just the sight of him reminded me I wasn't woman enough to help a man I'd loved." She was going to cry, but fought it back.

"You know," she said, trying to smile, "in one way, he was like you."

"How was that?" I asked, interested to know we had something besides Monica in common.

"Dedication. He was in love with the TV industry, the same way you are. Passionately. Like it was his family and his alma mater all in one."

"Do you know a man named Vern Devlin?" I asked.

"Not all that well. He works in the same department as Vince."

Since the only way I'd ever seen Vince was dead, her slip into the present tense for him seemed bizarre. I suppressed a shudder. "What do you know about him?"

"Not that much, really. He ran the football pool at CRI, went to the track with Vince a few times. He was a bad influence on Vince, I thought."

"They got along all right, though?"

"Yes, I suppose so. Vince would have told me if they'd quarreled, the way he told me everything else."

I realized there was something very important I didn't know. "What exactly did your husband do for CRI?"

"He was in charge of ARGUS."

"ARGUS." I was puzzled.

"Don't you know about ARGUS?" She might have been asking me if I knew who Jimmy Carter was.

"I assume you don't mean the Greek guy with a hundred eyes," I said.

She looked thoughtful. "How clever," she said. "Now I know how they got the name. ARGUS is the computer, the one that does the ratings for TV. It stands for Audience Research General Utilization System. He helped develop it. You know how it monitors all those sets at once?"

"ARGUS. A hundred eyes. Naturally," I said.

Monica said, "Anything else?"

"Yeah. Walter Schick. Name mean anything to you?"

She thought it over for a second. "Wasn't he a big shot

at the Network—yours I mean—who got killed or something?"

"Or something. Right. How do you know him?" You would be amazed at some of the things actors don't know about television.

"I think Vince mentioned him a few times. There was a big presentation at CRI to sell the networks on ARGUS, and I think Vince met him there; Schick was representing your Network."

"When was this?"

"Oh, just before Vince and I were married. You must know when the Network started using ARGUS," she said.

"Well yeah, but we just call them the *overnights*." A horrible thought dashed across the surface of my mind like a cockroach looking for a place to hide. I pinned it down and took a look at it.

"Monica, does Devlin talk like this?" I gave her a sample of Devlin's gargles-with-peanut-butter baritone. I'm good at impressions, and I wanted to be very sure I'd spoken to the real Vern Devlin.

"That's pretty close," she said, surprised. "How do you know how he sounds?"

"I know a lot of things I'd be better off not knowing, Dumpling." It slipped out. I hadn't called her Dumpling for a long time. I hoped she hadn't noticed, but I was sure she had.

I stood up, started to say good-bye.

"You're not leaving!" she said.

"It's almost one-thirty," I told her, "and I have to be at the office tomorrow. I'm sore, and depressed, and confused, and I need some sleep."

She was furious. "I threw a man out of my bed for you!"

I stopped with my hand on the knob, asking myself life's two Great Questions: "Why me?" and "What do I do *now*?" I couldn't come up with an answer for either one of them. I dropped my hand and turned to face her. She was standing with her hands on her hips, eyes wide, nostrils flared.

She couldn't keep it up. She sobbed. Her lip started to quiver, and she ran to me, clung to me. She was trembling.

I put my arms around her. She raised her face to me. The reflection from the lamp made her tears look golden, as though her eyes were melting and running down her face. I kissed her.

To hell with everything, I thought, to hell with the dead man, and the Network, and the truth about Walter Schick, *whatever* it was. I was holding Monica again, feeling her tongue like honeyed fire on mine again, so to hell with ratings, and Lieutenant Martin, and Tom Falzet, too.

But even before I finished thinking that, I knew it was nonsense, that I had to get out of there. Loving Monica was like being addicted to heroin, needing something all the time you know it's killing you. And I had responsibilities to all those people I had dispatched to hell a few seconds ago.

It took more willpower than I thought I had, but I forced my hands to stop and pulled them away from Monica. I separated us, gently. She backed away, looking hurt and bewildered.

I let myself out. Outside, I walked east to Broadway, and got a cab downtown.

Hindsight always works better than foresight, and mine was in rare form in that cab going home. I was telling myself I never should have goaded Carlson into giving me those little teasers of what he wanted to talk about. I could close my eyes and see it like a blurb on the cover of a cheap fan magazine: "The Awful Truth About Walter Schick!!!"

Leaving Schick out of it, there was a nice neat scenario of the murder. Carlson is a gambler, deep in debt. He can't pay. Gamblers (or loan sharks) are miffed. Gamblers (or loan sharks) have Carlson killed, or maybe do it themselves, just to keep their hand in. Beautifully compact. I hoped the police liked it, because that's what I'd left for them.

For myself, I'd reserved the ineluctable joy of fitting Walter Schick into the picture somewhere. Was he a gambler who had similarly backed himself into a corner and been dealt with? Possibly, but only barely. For one thing, there was no evidence Walter Schick was a gambler, let alone a compulsive one. That's not a thing that comes upon a man all of a sudden, and I was sure Mr. Hewlen would have noticed the signs and eased him out of the Network long ago. For another, even if he *had* been like that, and a compulsive loser besides, it would still be a real feat to get rid of *all* the money he had access to: what he had made himself and what his wife had secondhand from Mr. Hewlen.

After that, any theory I could come up with took me into the realm of the occult. Had Walter Schick killed Carlson? Not breathing with the aid of a respirator and curled up in a fetal position the way he had been for the last six months, he hadn't. Could Walter Schick have been one of the gamblers (or loan sharks) that Carlson was in debt to?

Never, despite how many 1930s movie serials you may have seen. Rich businessmen do not become racketeers just to make more money. Racketeers become businessmen in order to *keep* more money. And this is granting three things: that Schick had a secret, that he knew Carlson knew it, and that it was worth killing to keep.

I could hardly wait until Thursday. I hoped Devlin would show up. It wasn't my fault the police found out about him, he had plenty of time to hang up the phone. I'd be at Penn Station Thursday morning. Even if he couldn't tell me everything, as he promised, he could certainly tell me *something*.

The cab dropped me off in front of the palatial beehive I called home. Bart, the night doorman, was at his post. He could be more cheerful at two A.M. than anyone I ever heard of.

"Late night, eh, Mr. Cobb?" Some of my fellow tenants sometimes looked at me a little funny, as though they could smell a lack of money on me, but Bart was always friendly.

"Too damn late, if you ask me," I said. "How's it going, Bart?"

"Oh, 'bout the same, 'bout the same. Had a little excitement couple of hours ago, though. Heard a gal screaming around the corner. Went to look, but nobody was there."

"You took a big chance," I informed him. "That sounds like a classic setup."

He laughed, a big, deep chuckle. "Don't worry about me, Mr. Cobb. It hasn't been so long since I was going fifteen rounds twice a month. For less money than I make here, if you count tips.

"Besides, this uniform's got big pockets, and I just naturally keep them filled up a little."

He pulled one of his pockets open and pointed inside at a nasty-looking little automatic. I didn't blame him for having it. If I had to stand out on the sidewalk all night, between the possessions of a couple of hundred rich people and maybe a million junkies, I'd have one, too.

I told Bart good night, and took the elevator upstairs. I took out my keys, then stopped for a second when I heard a faint click from around the corner of the hall. It was the sound of the fire exit door closing. I didn't like that. This high up in the building, no one would *think* of using the fire stairs. Some of my neighbors are so spoiled, they wouldn't think of it even if there really were a fire.

There was a sound of rapid footsteps thumping on the carpet. They sounded too heavy to belong to the little guy who had tailed me outside Police Headquarters. I picked up the pace of my own steps, and shuffled through the keys to make sure the right one was handy.

The door to Rick and Jane's apartment was just around the next bend. When the footsteps behind me stopped, I could picture just what my playmate was up to. He'd gotten some woman to lure Bart away from the door (there are women in New York who will do *anything* for money), sneaked inside, and come up to this floor. People worry about Siberian tigers becoming extinct. What about elevator operators? I would feel a lot better if I were being followed by a guy who had just climbed eighteen flights of stairs.

Once he was up here, of course, all he'd had to do was wait in the stairwell with the door open a crack until I came up, and follow me, staying one bend behind so I couldn't see him.

He was waiting now, just around the corner, for me to unlock the door. Then he could jump me, drag me inside, and kill me, or worse, at his leisure.

From around the corner, I heard another click. It wasn't the fire door. The subject of switchblade knives was very fresh in my mind.

I thrust the key into the lock. I had to get that door open before Spot betrayed his presence. I turned the key with my right hand, the knob with my left, smashing my shoulder against the door at the same time. Spot's first bark was just escaping his throat.

I could feel the intruder behind me. I dove for the floor, rolling sideways to avoid the thrust of a knife. Only it wasn't a knife I'd heard click, it was a bullet being jacked into the chamber of an automatic. It caught the hall light and winked obscenely.

As I hit the floor, I yelled, "Take him, Spot!"

Those were the magic words that turned the mild-mannered house pet into three and a half feet of pure nastiness. Rick Sloan had sunk a lot of money into attack training for Spot, and I hoped it had been worth it.

He flew by me now, snarling, a snowball with teeth. I saw the attacker as a silhouette in the doorway. He looked enormously tall, but he was probably about the same height as me, though he must have outweighed me by fifty pounds of muscle. I couldn't make out any details about him except the gun and his blond hair.

He brought the gun up and snapped off a wild shot that missed Spot by a mile but came very near to taking my ear off. Then Spot was upon him. That feisty mutt went straight for the gun arm and latched onto it like a maniacal marshmallow. The gunman screamed in pain, and dropped the gun. Spot pulled him to the left, out of the frame of the doorway and out of my sight.

All of this took place in about one point seven seconds, but most serious fights don't take much longer. Spot had taken him by surprise, and turned the advantage from the gunman to me. I rolled over one more time, pulled my feet under me, and dashed out into the hall.

I was just in time to see Spot's pads as he tore around the corner in pursuit of his quarry, who had broken away. Spot was tough, but he wasn't a Doberman, by any means. The gunman had probably outweighed him by two hundred pounds. I took a split second to pick up the gun, and joined the chase.

When I caught up, I found Spot scratching at the elevator doors and snarling.

"Okay, boy," I said. "Cool it, Spot, he got away." The Samoyed immediately became his old, comical self again, prancing back to the apartment. I didn't pay much attention. I was thinking how lucky the blond gorilla had been that the elevator happened to be at this floor. Then I realized I had just gotten off it, and it wasn't likely to have been called away at two o'clock in the morning.

It wasn't until I was back inside, and had trouble locked out (I hoped), that the full weight of the realization that somebody had tried to kill me, *to kill me*, for Christ's sake, really sank in. I called Spot over to me, scratched his throat. "Good dog," I said, wiping away fear-sweat. "*Goddam* good dog." He licked my face and grinned at me.

I made a fool of myself over that dog that night. Anybody seeing me would have thought I was auditioning for the Roddy McDowall part in a remake of *Lassie, Come Home*.

I'd been saving a steak for a special occasion. I took it out of the refrigerator and put it in Spot's dish, and fixed a bowl of Cocoa Crispies and bananas for myself.

45

Spot tore into the steak. "Don't chew with your mouth open," I told him, but he didn't pay any attention. I sat down to eat my cereal.

I have a mind like a tar pit. Things hit the surface, stick, then sink and disappear. Then, after an indefinite period of time, they bubble to the top again, sometimes perfectly preserved, sometimes altered, sometimes stuck to something else.

That's what happened this time. I had just put some cereal in my mouth when a combination of a memory and a thought surfaced, sticking together.

The memory was of the phone call I'd taken from Devlin in the hotel room, and the thought was the one I'd had about the scream that had gotten the doorman out of the way: There are women in New York who'll do anything for money; any act, thought, or word. Like a scream, for example. Or maybe just to say fifteen words on the telephone.

The guy at the door had been a complication, something that would have to be dealt with. But I had the happy thought I could now deal with the *big* complication.

I was anxious to talk to Lieutenant Martin. If I could help him get his case solved, I'd have the NYPD off my back.

And I was also anxious to see Vern Devlin, more now than ever. I was betting he was the one who had killed Vince Carlson.

> *"Man . . . woman . . . birth . . . death . . . infinity."*
>
> —Sam Jaffe, "Ben Casey" (ABC)

7

I was up early the next morning. The first thing I did after I brushed my teeth was call Homicide South and ask for Lieutenant Martin. They told me to wait.

I glanced at the morning papers. The *News* had devoted its front page to a revelation about a crooked politician (a "Dog Bites Man" story if there ever was one) and had the murder of Carlson well back, on the same page with a record store ad. The *New York Times* found the story unfit to print. Apparently, the cops were still saving the details, or the papers would be going crazy over the TV tie-in. When was the last time you read any, *any* good word about the American television system? They hate us; newspapers, magazines, critics, all take their turn. Why? Beats me. The American viewer gets more programming, more variety, and more service than any TV viewer anywhere, for free.

Critics will say England does it better. But England imports far more of our programs than we do of theirs, however fine they are. Critics will say television should be a force for raising the public consciousness; in other words for telling the public neither more nor less than the critics feel it should be told.

I think *that's* the real gripe the critics have about American television. A critic is by definition an elitist; he lends us poor slobs the benefits of his superior taste. But television is the last Great Democracy. No government bureaucrat or cultural arbiter can decide what you watch. American television is the most successful medium of mass communication in the history of the world, and everybody counts. You cast your vote by means of an on-off switch or a tuner. And if you choose to watch a tenth rerun of

"Gilligan's Island," and I want to watch "60 Minutes," more power to both of us.

As I sat there developing this beautiful polemic, I regretted I had no one to deliver it to. I was going to look for something to write it down with, but had to give it up because there was somebody on the phone.

"What do you want, Cobb?" It was the voice of Detective Rivetz.

"Where's Lieutenant Martin?"

"What's the matter? Don't you think a cop is entitled to a little sleep?"

"No, it's not that," I said. "I want to tell him something."

"What?" he said with heavy sarcasm. "Hell, I can take your confession as well as he can."

Nobody out-sarcastics Matt Cobb at seven-thirty in the morning. "All right, I confess. He's living in my apartment, disguised as a dog."

"Who?" A natural straight man.

"Judge Crater," I said. "Now, if you will knock off the Pontius Pilate routine, I'll tell you why I called."

"I'm listening."

"I have to go up to Connecticut today for a few hours. Business."

"You interrupted my cup of coffee for that?" He sounded irate.

"Well, Lieutenant Martin asked me not to leave town."

Rivetz spoke very quietly. "Look, Cobb. You can go to Outer Mongolia for all I care. I ain't ready for you yet, but when I am, I'll find you. Don't worry about that."

"Goody!" I gushed. "Now tonight I can sleep all comfy-cozy!"

Rivetz made a noise before he slammed the receiver down. I think it was "Grr!"

"Up yours," I said, trying to get it in before the connection went. I wondered what Rivetz had against me. I was a nice guy; at least I thought so. I would be glad when I told Lieutenant Martin my idea and got the whole thing over with. I didn't dare try to tell Rivetz anything.

I got dressed and went downtown. I had an idea that, while my idea was great, evidence would be even better. At the Tower of Babble, I went first to my office to consult a couple of phone books, then back down to the twelfth floor.

I wanted to have a word or two with Millie Heywood in

Network Operations. Millie was a salty dame of about fifty, who was five feet tall on the tallest day of her life. She had joined the Network when female technicians were about as common as purple gorillas in the Mormon Tabernacle Choir. She knows more about the technical details of networking than anybody in the business.

I found her, as usual, surrounded by blinking lights and patch racks, delivering an opinion, loudly, of the intelligence, sanitary habits, and ancestry of a hapless technician about three times her size.

". . . and we'll test the goddam regional split when I *say* it's time to test the goddam regional split!" She took a breath. "And another thing, you—Cobb, get the hell out of here!"

"I missed you, too, Millie." I picked her up, threw her over my shoulder, and carried her to her private office. She showed me how much she liked it by hitting my back with her little fists.

I put her down at the door of her office. She took off her harlequin glasses and let them dangle by the string around her neck. That's how I knew she wasn't mad. When she was mad, they got pushed up to the top of her head.

"This is sexual harassment, you bastard! I'll get the Attorney General after you."

I looked at her in mock seriousness. "Okay, Millie, I promise I'll never do it again."

"No?" She sounded disappointed. "You better, you stinker. It's disgusting, but it breaks up the week. I've got everybody around here so buffaloed, they're afraid to ask me what time it is."

"Lot of new ones, huh?"

"Yeah. All the experienced guys are doing remotes, or took jobs as chief engineers at some hick station."

"Why don't you ease up a little on the kids?"

"And lose my reputation?" She had a point. A top technician is like a good left-handed relief pitcher. You need them, so you allow them a certain degree of flakiness. Millie's flakiness expressed itself in a nonstop tirade that was more bark than bite.

"They'll see through me sooner or later," she said. "They always do. Now, little boy, what can Aunt Millie do to get you out of her hair?"

I handed her a slip of paper with three phone numbers on it.

"I need a small favor," I said. "I'd appreciate it if you would contact one of your numerous admirers in the phone company, preferably in long lines, and find out what time last night a call was placed from either of these two numbers to this number, in New York."

"Where are these other two numbers from?" she asked.

"Washington, D.C., and Fairfax, Virginia."

She looked at me suspiciously. "Why?" she asked.

"Don't ask."

"It's more of that dirty stuff, isn't it? That fag actor is in trouble again, isn't he? Look here, I don't mind doing a little favor, but—"

I cut her off before she built up a head of steam, and assured her the famous leading man to whom she had referred was behaving himself commendably. It took a while, but she finally bought it. I thanked her, and left.

I was feeling pretty jaunty, because I had decided that Devlin had killed Carlson. That call was a fake, I was sure, designed to make me trust him, and not spill what Carlson had told me to the cops. *He* had no way of telling how much I knew. After I walked in on him, he knocked me out, paid some hooker to pretend to be an operator, and bingo! a long-distance phone call. Lord knew it wasn't hard to find a hooker in that neighborhood.

He was fast, but not smart. All long-distance calls are registered by a computer, to be itemized on the bill later. Devlin's call had ostensibly been person-to-person, so the live operator who had been on duty could back the computer up when Millie's contact (as I was sure he would) reported that *no* call had been placed from either CRI or Devlin's house to the Hotel Cameron.

I figured naming the killer would go a long way toward helping the police forget my falsified statement.

But what about Walter Schick? I persisted in asking myself. I *still* had to know what awful secret endangered the whole Network and even the industry itself. That's why I had more than one thing to do in Connecticut.

Upstairs at Special Projects, I told Jazz I was going out to take care of the Kenny Lewis situation.

She looked worried. "But Mr. Falzet said—"

"So Falzet's got you keeping an eye on me."

"No, I just don't want you to get in trouble."

"I can worry about myself, Jazz," I said. "Remember, he can't fire you unless he fires me first."

"Okay." She grinned.

"Hold the fort until I get back. I'm expecting a couple of calls. Take a message from Millie Heywood, but tell Jack Hansen I'll call him back. Get a number."

"Sure thing. Anything else?"

"Yes, don't go into Falzet's office alone, no matter what he tells you."

I left her blushing.

The very basement of NetHQ is a garage. I stopped there next and checked out a car. As usual, it was less a car than it was a yacht. Mr. Hewlen had the idea that if an executive, even a very junior executive, were to be seen in anything smaller than an Oldsmobile, the image of the Network would suffer irreparable damage.

This particular number was unmarked, but it was done up in the Network's favorite color scheme, black outside, white inside. You haven't lived until you've maneuvered a dinosaur like that out of a cellar garage onto Sixth Avenue at ten o'clock in the morning.

I had the Kenny Lewis thing finished by twelve-thirty. I couldn't help feeling sorry for that kid, even though he was a worthless punk. What chance did he have? All his life, he'd been taken care of, no matter what, and no one would tell him why. If his famous mother set out to deliberately drive him insane, she couldn't have done a better job. She wouldn't acknowledge the kid, or even see him; she just couldn't be bothered. The whole thing made me a little nauseated.

My next destination was Willowdale private hospital in Greenwich. From the outside, it was the place of my dreams: a rambling, peaceful white house, with a pillared porch and gravel drive, surrounded by a pool-table lawn and shaded by willows and chestnut trees. It looked like a place where no one ever talked loud or sweated.

The illusion was shattered the moment I stepped inside. Doctors and nurses rushed by on their rounds, and antiseptic perfumed the air. The only perceptible difference between Willowdale and Bellevue was the shape of the windows.

An elderly lady volunteer at the desk was making clucking noises over a paperback novel. "Such filth!" she muttered, shaking her head. She marked her place with a finger while she told me the way to Walter Schick's room. As I left her, she resumed clucking.

A young guy in a white suit was coming out of the room as I was going in, and we bumped into each other.

"Excuse me," I said. "Are you a doctor?"

He grinned. "That's what they have to call me. I'm the intern."

"Hi. Matt Cobb." He told me he was Fred Barber, and we shook hands.

"Is anything wrong with Mr. Schick?" I asked.

He scratched his head. "Well, yeah. He had an accident—"

"No, no. Sorry, I phrased the question stupidly. I meant, I saw you coming out of the room, and I wondered if something had changed."

"Oh," he said, "I get you. No, I just dropped in to bring Mrs. Schick something from the desk."

"She's here?" Sometimes, I can't say anything that isn't stupid.

He ignored it. "She sure is. Every day, hours at a time. She doesn't even bring a book, just sits there and looks at him. I think we'll wind up treating *her*, too. We can't do anything for him. Maybe you can cheer her up a little."

I told him I'd try, and walked in the room. Cynthia Schick stood up, looking almost startled.

"Mr. Cobb," she said. "How nice of you to come." She was a very attractive woman. Only a few neck cords and some highlights of grey in her black hair betrayed the fact that she had told forty good-bye. She was taller than her father, Mr. Hewlen, but had his flinty blue eyes and determined mouth. To borrow a phrase from Jane Russell, she was a full-figured girl, and that figure would have been an asset to a woman half her age.

She was much more subdued now than I'd ever known her before. Usually, she was the crisp and efficient female executive type, the kind of well-to-do lady who gave more than her name to charity projects; the kind who works as hard to give money away as most people do to earn it.

"Hello, Mrs. Schick," I said. "I'd like to talk to you, if you don't mind."

She didn't answer right away. It's only good manners to keep your eyes on the person to whom you are speaking, but mine kept being drawn to the patient on the bed.

When I had known him, Walter Schick had been the classic executive, the perfect complement to his wife. He had been a mover and shaker at the Network and throughout the industry. When his daughter had run away, he'd been impressive even in his helplessness.

What lay on the bed was a caricature of the man, a five-foot, ten-inch infant with a beard stubble on his face. He resembled Walter Schick a little bit.

He was being kept alive through the combined efforts of several pharmaceutical companies and by Connecticut Light and Power. Medicines and nutrients were being fed into him by needles stuck into veins of both wrists. Electronic equipment maintained and monitored the rhythms of his body the way Net Ops maintains and monitors the quality of a broadcast signal. His chest rose and fell in rhythm with the cylindrical bellows on the respirator beside the bed.

The silence became thunderous. I said something only to hear a human voice.

"How long have you been here with your husband today, Mrs. Schick?"

She looked at me calmly. "That's not my husband," she said.

Do you want to know the truth about Walter Schick? Carlson's voice echoed in my head.

"It's not?" I asked. My voice cracked, but Cynthia Schick took no notice of it.

"What is a man?" she said. "Surely Matthew Cobb is something more than a tall, handsome young man in a three-piece suit. Walter was action, decision and action. Spirit, Mr. Cobb, and *ideas. That* was my husband. I haven't seen him since the accident."

She pointed to the bed. "This is what he's left behind."

"Yet the intern tells me you come here every day."

She showed me a joyless smile. "Yes, I do. Sometimes I wonder why. It's like adoring a relic of a saint. Walter was a good man, but he wasn't a saint."

"Why then?"

"I think it's because I hope to be here, when . . . it . . . Walter returns to . . ." She pointed again. The figure on the bed made a gurgling sound.

"I'm very glad you've come, Mr. Cobb. I sit here alone, thinking things, keeping them locked up . . . sometimes I start feeling as though *I'm* the one who's being punished. I need to get some things said. You don't mind . . . ?"

"Not at all. I'm probably just the right person to tell it to."

She looked at me strangely. "What do you . . . ? Oh, I

53

think I see. You're outside the immediate family, yet you know things about us that no one else knows. Is that what you meant?"

"That," I said, "and the fact that I got a real good feeling when I heard Roxanne was off drugs and back in school. It's a privilege to help a family with courage."

She went white at that. "It's strange you should mention that, Mr. Cobb. About courage, I mean. Because I've been so confused!" She left her chair, and stood between the respirator and the window, looking outside.

"The sky is getting cloudy," she said. She turned to face me.

The respirator was between us. She seemed hypnotized by the rising and falling of the cylinder with the patient's breath. "Sometimes I wonder if it wouldn't be better if . . ." Her voice trailed off.

She was stroking something. I stood up to see what it was. She was holding the power cord for the respirator. One good yank, and the last of Walter Schick would die.

"Mrs. Schick," I said.

She looked up, startled. "Yes?"

"Put that down, Mrs. Schick."

"Don't you see, Mr. Cobb, that's the problem. I just don't know if I have the courage to do this." She took a firmer grip on the cord.

"It takes more courage not to do it," I said, "and you know it."

Tears were on her cheeks, her voice was a whisper. "He's never coming back," she said.

Why can't I ever go visit anybody anymore? I asked myself. Spot was the only person I hadn't had a crisis with in two days.

I was not anxious to see her pull that plug. Whatever *you* call it, the State of Connecticut would call it premeditated murder. Of course, I could immobilize Mrs. Schick with one hand, but I had to reach her first, and it would have taken a standing broad jump over the bed to reach her before she could act.

"But what if you've got it wrong?" I said suddenly.

"What do you mean?"

"You say he's away; that whatever is Walter, his mind, his *soul,* is gone and only the shell is left behind. But what if he's not away? *What if he's only trapped?* Trapped, way deep inside, so deep he can't get out? Or at least, not yet. What if he's . . . if he's a *prisoner* in his own body?"

"A prisoner?" she asked thoughtfully.

"Of course! And what you're thinking of doing is to burn down the prison, with your husband inside! Even the worst murderer gets treated better than that, Mrs. Schick. Don't do it to your husband."

Then she did something so bizarre, it had to be genuine. She dropped the wire, composed her face, brushed the dirt from her hands and said, "You're quite right, Mr. Cobb. Thank you."

And that was it. I was dumbfounded. I was steeling myself for the Hollywood finish, the fainting, or the body-wracking sobs, and what I got seemed like an anticlimax. Nobody could fake a thing like that.

She picked up her purse. "Can I impose on you one more time, Mr. Cobb? Roxanne drove me here, and I'd rather not wait for her to come back. If I call her, would you drive me home?"

". . . the life you save may be your own."
—National Safety Council,
public service announcement

I knew the way there. I pointed the car in the right direction and headed for the other side of Greenwich, the Sound shore. After a while, I said, "Mrs. Schick, I have to ask you some questions you probably don't want to hear."

She shrugged. "I can hardly refuse you, can I?" I wasn't sure what she meant by that.

"I want to know about your husband's accident."

"My God, why?"

"Safety study for the Personnel Department," I lied. "Just tell me what happened. January eleventh, right? He went out alone?"

"Yes, he went out alone. That was the night we had a terrible ice storm. Roxanne was home from college, on semester break, and she had gone to a friend's house earlier in the evening, you know how the children can't wait to see each other and compare notes at the end of a term.

"The storm hit after Roxanne had gone. She called just after eleven o'clock. She said she heard the roads were impassable, and that power lines were down, and she didn't know what to do.

"She said she was to afraid to drive. Walter told her not to worry, he'd pick her up right away. He took the Mercedes because it was the easiest car to get to.

"After he drove off, the next time I saw him, he was . . . the way he is now. A state policeman came to the door and told me Walter had been in an accident, and brought me to the hospital."

"Not Willowdale?" I asked.

"What? Oh, no. Greenwich Hospital." She was silent for a few seconds, then said, without expression, "One of the doctors told me he was lucky to be alive."

"Where was this, exactly?"

56

"We'll be coming to that stretch of road in a few moments, now," she said.

We were on a road built along the top of a ridge, with a steep drop of about fifteen feet to either side. Mrs. Schick said, "The police decided he must have hit a patch of ice and skidded off the road. They said he'd been driving too fast. The car rolled over several times, and Walter wasn't wearing his seat belt. He was injured all over, but, of course, his head was the worst."

"Did he usually wear his seat belt?"

She hesitated. "Not always," she said after a couple of seconds.

Famous last words, I thought. It was time for the big money question, but I waited before asking it; I didn't want to disturb her. But she looked pretty well in control of herself, so I let it rip.

"Was there any suspicion it wasn't an accident?"

"The police didn't think so." Her tone indicated how much she thought of the opinion of the police.

"Did they mention it at all?"

"Oh, they mentioned it. They said it had to be an accident, because there were no other car tracks to show he'd been forced off the road, and no traces of a person on foot who might have distracted him."

That was good enough for me. I'd stop by the State Police barracks and have a word or two with one of the officers, but I was satisfied. Still, Carlson had been killed trying to tell me *something*, and I had placed myself in a position where I couldn't afford not to know it. I pressed on.

"Did—does your husband have any enemies?" I cursed myself for forgetting Walter Schick was still alive.

"You were right the first time, Matt. My husband has no enemies *now*."

"In other words, you're saying he used to?"

"Any man who marries the boss's daughter is going to have enemies," she declared. "Any man of talent and ambition is going to have enemies, especially in an industry as competitive as ours. Yes, Walter had enemies."

"Who, for instance?"

"Do you really want me to say it?"

"Say whatever you think."

She gave me a look that told me I asked for it, and said, "Tom Falzet."

57

Tom Falzet. Great. I felt like Pandora with hair on her chest. Every time I asked somebody something, another demon flew out of the box. Now I was sweating the last *two* Network Presidents.

"Tom was always afraid of Walter," she said. "When Walter was in charge of Sales, and Tom in charge of Programming, they were always trying to outdo each other. They both knew one of them would be picked as President when my father stepped upstairs.

"You know, Matt, my birth was an accident."

That called for a double take. "Most are," I said.

"What I mean is, my father was already an old man when I was born. He'd poured all his love into the Network. *That's* what he built his life around. He would *never* have favored a man at the Network simply because he was married to me. And it *should* be like that.

"But Tom Falzet used it *against* Walter, joked about it, subtly, of course, but he always kept Father aware that if Walter were to be named President, everyone would assume it was because of me.

"Walter was the best man for the job. Tom knew it, and Father knew it, too. If it weren't for the whispers, the insinuations, Father would have stepped aside for Walter years ago. That's why Father remained active head of the Network so long. I'm sure you know how he is. He wouldn't tolerate anyone but the best man running the Network, but it would kill him to have the people in the industry say he was unfair."

"But then 'Harbor Heights' came along," I suggested.

Cynthia Schick nodded. She probably knew the details better than I did, but everyone who worked in the Tower had heard of it. It was one of the biggest intramural battles in the history of the broadcasting industry.

It has to do with the critics I talked about earlier, and their comments on broadcast programming.

Now, nobody likes to be attacked daily in a newspaper. I'll bet even Charles Manson didn't like it. Tom Falzet liked it least of all. He was in charge of Programming at the time, and bore the brunt of the attacks.

So one day, he came up with an idea to get the critics to lay off: namely, to design a show expressly to please the critics. "Harbor Heights" was born.

Hell broke loose. Walter Schick was against it from the first. To him would fall the task of convincing advertisers to invest their advertising budgets in the show. He maintained it couldn't be done, that the public didn't want that kind of show and had made its opinion clear time after time. He further maintained that if he and his staff *did* manage to get it sold, the folks who paid the bills (advertisers) would be feeling betrayed when "Harbor Heights" bombed, as it inevitably would.

The whole Tower was kept in suspense. Everybody from Top Management down to the janitor's assistants speculated about what Mr. Hewlen's decision would be.

The word finally came down. With nose firmly uplifted, the Network would introduce "Harbor Heights" with the new fall season.

Looking back from the end of that season, it was now easy to see that the old man put it on the air to see who had the right hunches to be President.

The first episode of "Harbor Heights" made the critics swoon with joy. It had everything they like: rich people, upper-class accents, oh-so-tasteful sex, and "relevance." It opened with a good rating, too, a 40 share in the CRI ratings. That means forty percent of all the television sets in use that Sunday night were tuned to "Harbor Heights."

That's a terrific number. It means the show got a good sampling with the audience. They can't like it if they don't try it.

The next week, the share had dropped to 26, though Neilsen and Arbitron did show it a little higher. They'd tried it, but they didn't like it.

By the end of another two weeks, the share was down to 16. Cancellation rumors flew, but Falzet hung tough. "Harbor Heights" was moved to Friday. The ratings dropped again.

After eight shows, "Harbor Heights" was cancelled. Seven percent of the viewing public watched the last episode, which aired late in October.

Early in November, Walter Schick was named President of the Network. In mid-January, he was put in that bed in Willowdale, half dead.

I regarded the half widow. "Do you think Tom Falzet was so angry about his failure, and your husband's promotion, that he tried to have him killed?"

"I would have no trouble believing it," she said.

"Okay," I said. "Could you believe Roxanne conspired with him to do it?"

"That's a disgusting thought!" she snapped.

"I agree," I said. "That's why I don't think it was anything but an accident. Even if someone, say Falzet, had a way to make Walter go off the road, how could he get him there in the first place? It was your daughter's call that got him out of the house, and it's ridiculous to think she'd have been a party to anything like that."

I changed the subject. "Does your husband know a man named Vincent Carlson?"

"No!" she snapped, then, more quietly, "not to my knowledge."

"Vernon Devlin?"

"Again, not that I know of. Why?"

"A vagrant thought. Never mind."

We arrived at the Schick residence, a modern flagstone-and-glass affair built on a bluff overlooking Long Island Sound. I drove the car under the carport. Cynthia Schick invited me in. "Roxanne will be happy to see you," she said.

I wanted to see her, too. I accompanied Mrs. Schick inside the house. The living room was walled with glass on three sides, and the numerous potted trees and shrubs inside gave me the feeling of being on display in a terrarium. A middle-aged lady in a grey uniform was giving the south wall a Windex treatment, and the droplets of spray made the Sound and the hazy shape of Long Island beyond look like a mirage.

"Roxanne!"

I was startled to hear Mrs. Schick yell like that. I've always had F. Scott Fitzgerald's attitude about the rich—that they're different from you and me. I don't know how I expected Mr. Hewlen's descendants to act: maybe they sent each other telegrams.

"Roxanne!" she called again. To the maid, she said, "Agatha, have you seen my daughter?"

"I think she went down to the beach, Ms. Schick." I couldn't tell if the Ms. was Women's Lib talk or a slurred Mrs.

"No problem," I said. "How do I get down to the beach?"

Mrs. Schick told the maid to show me the way. Agatha took me to a long flight of wooden stairs in back of the house that led down a bluff to a strip of sand between the rocky bottom of the hill and the green waters of the Sound.

Roxanne was lying on a blanket, on her back with one

knee bent, possibly asleep. My footsteps made no noise on the sand as I approached her. She had her eyes closed, and was unaware of me. I just looked at her for a couple of seconds.

Three years ago, when I had walked into a tin-roofed shack in Albany, New York, I'd found a pale, sick, scared little girl with arms and legs that looked like route maps for the Penn Central.

Now those arms and legs were clean; sleek and brown their whole length. The girl was sleek and brown all over, except where the blue work shirt tied under her chest gapped to show the creamy side of a young breast.

In that shirt, and in her frayed tan cutoffs, she looked as though she'd been washed ashore. The warm sun had made her skin shiny with sweat. Her dark hair spread in a perfect fan beneath her.

I was tempted to go away and let her sleep. I woke her as gently as I could, walking around her to block the sun from her face.

Her eyes popped open, then combined with her mouth to make a Ballantine three-ring sign. She came up to her knees and clapped her hands together rapidly, looking for all the world like a blue-eyed seal.

"Cobb!" she squealed. She jumped up to hug me.

"Hey, come on, Twerp," I protested, "you're bending the material."

She laughed, and sat back down, cross-legged, on the blanket. "I suppose that *was* a mite childish," she said.

"Some of my best friends are childish," I said. She had a right to act childishly. She'd been robbed of her own childhood.

"Well, take off that jacket, and sit down and talk to me, Cobb!" When I had complied, she said, "Well, what brings you into the wilds of Fairfield? I haven't seen you in *years!*"

"Six months," I said. I had paid my respects right after the accident.

She shook her head. "Can't you excuse a little hyperbole, for crying out loud? Heck, I even know the right figure of speech."

"Okay," I said, "what kind of figure of speech is 'for crying out loud'?"

She looked thoughtful for a second. "Schenectady?" she asked brightly.

I laughed. "Close enough. How's school?"

She shrugged. "It keeps me off the streets, and it keeps me out of Her Majesty's way."

After a while, she said, "You still haven't told me why you're here, Cobb."

"I drove your mother home from Willowdale."

"Visiting the vegetable, huh?"

"That's a pretty cold thing to say, Rox. When you took off, your father never told me, 'Go find the junkie.' "

She blushed. "I'm sorry, really. I just . . . I say things like that to show I can take it." She traced curves in the sand with her fingers.

"You don't have to prove anything to me, Rox," I said.

"To myself, I do. After all, it's all my fault."

"Kids say the darnedest things!"
—Art Linkletter, "House Party" (CBS)

9

Freud showed us that we can feel guilty for large numbers of bizarre reasons. We tend to forget we can still feel guilty because we *are* guilty. I hoped I would like the answers to the questions I was about to ask.

"Rox," I said, "we've been through a lot, right?"

She smiled. "Right. Barfing, and chills, and knife fights . . ."

"Ah, that was nothing. I could have handled that turkey with handcuffs on. *You* were the one that gave me trouble. I still have the scar where you bit me."

"I don't believe it," she said.

I raised my right hand. "Scout's honor. I still have to go for rabies shots."

She made a face. "You are a true bastard, Cobb."

"Of course. It's a prerequisite for employment, these days." I got serious. "Why is it your fault, Rox?"

"It always is," she said. "I give off disaster the way a firefly gives off light."

"Cut it out. Okay, I'll ask you this. Why didn't you stay overnight at your friend's house instead of asking your father to come and pick you up?"

She looked at me suspiciously. "Why?" she asked.

"Trust me, Rox."

" 'Trust me,' " she mimicked. " 'Trust me.' That's what you tell a girl before you fuck her."

"I think you know me well enough to know whose side I'm on, Roxanne." I said it rather stiffly. "Make up your mind, then tell me or not."

"I trust *you*," she said. "But am I talking to Matt Cobb, or am I talking to the Network?"

"Hey," I said. "Let's get this straight right away. I may

wear the uniform, but I've got my own number on my back. If you're in trouble, I'll try my best to help you out."

"See that, Cobb? Do you see what you're doing to me? What makes you think I'm in trouble?"

"*I* sure as hell don't know. *You're* the one who said it was all your fault. Then you get all bent out of shape when I try to find out what you're talking about!"

"Okay, okay," she said. "It's no big thing. At least it wasn't at the time. I was over at Frieda Treleng's house, and about ten-thirty, she shows me a sandwich bag full of grass and asks me to share it with her. Nobody around here knows about . . . before. I don't think Frieda would have brought it up if she'd known.

"I kept thinking things like, *this is where I came in.* I started to shake. And in spite of everything, I *wanted* to do it. I *wanted* to do it!"

She had drawn her knees up to her body and was rubbing her shins nervously.

"You can imagine how that made me feel about myself. Didn't I *know* I couldn't handle it? Didn't I remember how I wound up? It wasn't the grass itself—some people can take it in stride.

"But I made a promise to myself that I would never get high again on anything; dope, booze, anything. I found out how much I wanted to break that promise. I had to get out of there. If I stayed I would have smoked that dope with her, and I couldn't stand that. I have a hard enough time living with myself as it is.

"I would have taken my own car home, but there was a terrible ice storm that night. I didn't want to make Dad come out, but I *had* to get away!

"I wouldn't even wait in the house. I got my coat and stood out on the porch, freezing, waiting for Dad to show up. I got a policeman instead."

She hugged her knees tight to her and squeezed her eyes shut.

"I'm sorry, Rox," I said softly. "I had to know."

"Don't worry about it," she said, releasing herself to take the sun on her legs once more. "The only thing is, I had to drop Frieda. I only know one person up at school that doesn't drink or do drugs, and she's gay. I spend all my time locked up in my little room. I'll be an A student in spite of myself."

I took her hand. "Look," I said, "I know it's tough, but

you did the right thing by calling your father. Don't feel guilty about it."

She gave me a warm look. "Thanks, Cobb. And I won't feel guilty about the other thing, either."

"What other thing?"

She laughed again. "I'm only kidding. My mother has to carry that cross."

"What are you talking about?"

"The argument, of course. There had to be an argument. My father was a great driver; the *best* in the world. We couldn't ever keep a chauffeur because Dad would always criticize his driving. He wasn't the show-off kind of good driver; he was just proud of doing something perfectly.

"Except when he was upset and angry. Did you ever see him like that, Cobb?"

I had. His rage was awesome.

"Well, that's it. When he was in a fight, he forgot everything else. I wouldn't drive with him when he was like that. I would have that night, though," she added in a murmur.

"So I'm sure Dad and my mother must have had a brawl that I interrupted when I called. He *never* would have gone off that road any other way."

"What if someone deliberately tried to force him off?"

"I don't care." She was adamant. "I don't care if they sabotaged the car. He would have protected himself, somehow. Hell, the very fact he wasn't wearing a seat belt proves he was upset. He always put his seat belt on, except when he was angry."

"What could they have argued about?"

"Me," she said. "That's what they always argued about. My mother has never forgiven me for what I did, you know. She tries to hide it, especially now, but she thinks deep down that I'm an ungrateful little bitch."

I wanted to tell her she was mistaken, but I couldn't. Mother and daughter just were not too fond of each other. It's tragic, but it happens.

As a diversionary tactic, I tried a terrible old joke. "Don't swear, it sounds like hell."

Roxanne shook her head in mock sadness. "Oh Cobb, you are so hopeless," she lamented. "Such a square. Three-piece suits. Rescues damsels in distress. Death on drug pushers. Doesn't like cuss words."

She shook her head again, seriously, this time. "You're

much too good for the job you do. Do you know that, Cobb?"

"Well, yeah," I said, "but we don't have kings in this country, so I have to settle."

"Ha, ha," she said sarcastically. "But I know you, Cobb, probably as well as anybody. I've seen you in action. You try to come on hard-boiled, but you are strictly a thirty-second egg. You care too much. I remember when you—"

"Come on, Roxanne!" I broke in. "What is this, 'This Is Your Life'?"

"All right, I'll skip the testimonials. But what I want to say is this: Get out of it, Cobb. I only can imagine the kind of filth you have to deal with. And I'm speaking as an ex-filth. It's gonna wreck you. It's not a place for good guys, Cobb. I love my father, but he used to call himself the 'Gunslinger' and be proud of it."

I shook my head at her. "You're blowing it all up out of proportion," I said. "It's not as bad as all that, you'll find it in any business. Besides, I'm just going to do this until I can elbow my way back into News or Production. Then all I'll have to do is make shows."

"Do you actually think they'll let you? They love having you in Special Projects. You're Jiminy Cricket. You have a conscience. You filter all the garbage through it, and my grandfather, Falzet, and the Network stay clean. *Listen* to me, Cobb, I was *raised* in that damn Tower."

"I won't argue with you," I said. "But just what should I do to stave off moral destruction?"

"Please don't laugh at me, Cobb. I literally owe you my life; I'm trying to pay you back a little.

"Quit. Leave the Network. Become a corny old English teacher, the way you planned. Get yourself a woman, and worry about a *real* family, not a corporate monstrosity."

That looked like a good way to change the subject. "Who would have *me?*" I asked, joking.

She met my eyes, not joking, and said, "I would have you, Cobb."

It's the nicest thing anybody can say to you, if you think about it. I didn't know what to say.

For the second time in less than a day, a woman answered my thoughts as though I'd spoken them aloud. "You don't have to say anything," Roxanne told me. "You asked me a question and I answered it, period. I'm not a little girl. I'm a voting, taxpaying adult, *and* a major stockholder in the Network. And I haven't been a virgin since I was fourteen."

I've got this joke reflex. If I don't like the way the conversation is going, I automatically try to joke my way out, no matter how many times it takes. This time it finally worked. I told her *I* had probably been a virgin until she was fourteen, too.

"Bet you asked her to marry you," she said with a smile. "You're such a straight arrow, you'd feel obligated."

I said, "You're too goddam smart for your own good, Twerp." I stood up, and helped Roxanne to her feet. We walked to the stairway.

"Rox," I said as we started up the steps, "don't let your mother visit the hospital alone anymore, all right?"

"How come? I hate that place . . . I was stuck in there a long time myself, you know."

"Roxanne, I know you and your mother have problems, but she needs your help. If what you say about that argument problem is true, it means your mother is carrying around a heavier load of guilt than you are. It would explain what she almost did today."

She looked puzzled. "What did she almost do?"

"She almost pulled the plug on your father's respirator."

"Jesus," she said. "Oh, Jesus. She's been strange lately, but I never expected anything like *this*."

"Strange how? For how long?"

"Ever since the accident. She goes out at odd hours, she *jumps* on the phone when it rings, things like that. At first I thought she had a boyfriend, but it doesn't make sense. She loves Dad. That's the one thing we agree on."

"She might be better off if she *did* have a boyfriend," I blurted. I should know better than to think out loud. I apologized to Roxanne.

"No, I agree with you," she said. "Mother isn't old, and she's letting Dad's condition wreck her life. If she had somebody else, she wouldn't dwell on it so much."

Just before we went into the house, I asked Roxanne what the maid's last name was.

"Locker, Agatha Locker. Why do you ask?"

"Because, I'm going to talk to her, I don't want you to order her to talk me, I want her to talk freely. It will sound more respectful if I call her Mrs."

"We owe Agatha a lot," Roxanne said. "The night of the accident, when they brought me home, I was a total wreck.

67

Agatha held me and sang to me the way she did when I was a baby."

Cynthia Schick wasn't around when we went in. Roxanne went upstairs to take a look around for her. Agatha was vacuuming the dining room, and I went in there to talk to her.

"Mrs. Locker," I yelled over the whine of the machine.

"What?" she yelled back.

"I want to talk to you!"

"What?"

"Could you shut the vacuum cleaner off?"

"Wait a minute," she hollered, "let me shut the vacuum cleaner off!"

I can't hear you, I've got a banana in my ear, I thought. I was *living* bad jokes now.

The machine subsided, and conversation became possible.

"Mrs. Locker," I said. "I hate to interrupt your work, but I'd like to ask you a question, if you don't mind."

She looked indifferent. "Well, you can *ask,*" she said.

"Thank you. It's really a simple question. Did Mr. and Mrs. Schick have an argument the night of the accident?"

"No offense, Mr. . . . ?"

"Cobb. Matt Cobb." I apologized for not telling her right off who I was.

"No offense, Mr. Cobb, but it ain't none of your business." She said it with all the dignity she could muster, which was quite a bit.

I hemmed and hawed for a second. Mike Hammer never has trouble like that. Somebody doesn't answer the question, he punches them out. Mickey Spillane holds a kind of horrible fascination for me.

"Ordinarily, I wouldn't pry," I said, "but I work for the Network, and it's my job to investigate certain accusations people have made about Mr. Schick. My only interest is to find out the truth, and see that innocent people don't suffer."

"Like who?" she asked.

"I won't know who's innocent until I find out the truth, will I?" I asked with a smile.

She gave me a good hard look, as though she were scanning my soul for black spots. I tried to look honest.

Finally, she said, "Well, the Good Book says 'the Truth shall make you free.' "

I was in, now. "Yes ma'am," I said. "John, eighth chapter, thirty-second verse."

She beamed at me. "Now what was it you wanted to know?"

"Just if Mr. and Mrs. Schick argued that night."

"Well, yes, they did. I can't tell you what it was about, though. I was in my room, reading. They had their voices real loud, though, I could tell they were real mad."

"Did they have fights like that often?"

She considered her answer, as though afraid of giving me a wrong impression. "Well," she said, "arguing is a part of any marriage, Lord knows Locker and me had our share, rest his soul. But no, that night they were way louder than most times."

"Did you hear anything of the argument at all?"

"Nope—well, I guess I did at that. They left off the fighting for a while, I guess when Miss Schick called on the phone, then just before Mr. Schick left the house, he said, 'We better hope I *am* wrong!' Just like that, only he put the Lord's name to it, too. Then I heard the door slam."

I scratched my head. Bits and pieces. A mess, like a pizza with mushrooms and sausage but no crust; lots of tasty little tidbits, but nothing to hold it all together.

Agatha had been talking. "Excuse me?" I said.

"I asked you if that was all you wanted."

"Ah—yes. Thank you, you've been very helpful."

She kicked the Electrolux back to life. I left her and went back to the living room where Roxanne was waiting for me. She was talking to the plants. If that really works, we can solve the world's hunger problems just by playing tapes of political speeches to wheat fields. Just imagine what we'd save on fertilizer.

I was about to tell Roxanne good bye when the front door opened and Cynthia Schick walked in. You could feel the temperature drop.

"Oh, Matt," she said as she closed the door behind her. "I didn't know you were still here. I hope Roxanne has been keeping you amused."

"We've had a real ball, Mother." The claws were sharp on both of them. Evidently, they got in a lot of practice.

Roxanne said, "We wondered where you were."

"I had to deliver some of your father's things to the

69

insurance company's office. I'm sorry that I didn't consult you."

I hate cat fights. I broke in to say I'd be heading back to the city.

"Thank you for driving me home, Mr. Cobb. Please visit us again."

"I'll make it a point," I said.

She excused herself, and went upstairs. Roxanne walked me through the jungle of houseplants to the door. She looked right at home in her ragged outfit. "Good-bye, Cobb," she said. "I don't know what you're up to, but don't feel obliged to be a hero, okay?"

"Don't worry about me," I assured her. "I'm such a chicken, I was drafted on the first round by Frank Perdue."

I bent to give her an avuncular good-bye kiss on the forehead, but she moved, changing the target to her mouth, and responded in a very unniecelike way, so I broke it off, and went.

A stop at the nearest headquarters of the State Police removed the last vestige of doubt that Walter Schick had met with no foul play. They had done it up brown, and from every scientific vantage point, from metallurgy to meteorology, it was an accident.

Okay. So it was an accident. *That* wasn't the truth Walter Schick had hanging over him, and that Carlson was going to spill to me. I had no idea how to go looking for what it was.

And, as I was startled to realize, I didn't care anymore. I wanted this whole business off my back. I'd give Lieutenant Martin the story on Devlin, and keep my mouth shut otherwise. If the truth about Walter Schick was that important, it would come out eventually. I was tired of the whole bit. The Truth shall make you tired.

Having made my decision, I felt considerably better about things as I drove back to the Tower of Babble.

"What a revoltin' development this is!"
—William Bendix,
"The Life of Riley" (NBC)

10

I got back to NetHQ before the first wave of rush hour traffic swarmed the streets of Manhattan, so it was relatively easy to get the dinosaur stowed away.

Jazz had a whole list of things to tell me when I got back to the office.

"Jack Hansen called," she said. "He'll be down in the newsroom all afternoon. Harris called. He said he's dating a secretary from the Russian Embassy, and he's putting it on the expense account. He said to tell you he'll have our guys put up as guests of honor at the Kremlin before he's through."

I wouldn't put it past him. Harris Brophy is the freest spirit I ever met. I never saw anybody worry less and accomplish more.

"Did Millie Heywood call yet?" I asked.

"No, she didn't. I can check with her if you want."

"Yeah, do that. Anything else?"

"Yes. Lieutenant Martin of the police is waiting for you in your office."

"Damn it, Jazz, don't do that!" She had saved the blockbuster for last again, like a damn juggling act.

"Yes, sir. I won't do it again." We both knew she was lying. I could tell from the twinkle in her eye.

"How long has the lieutenant been here?"

"Fifteen minutes or so."

"Okay. No calls except from Millie, Jazz."

Lieutenant Martin had his nose buried in my SIK file (Scandals If Known) that's supposed to be under lock and key at all times. He was sitting in my chair with his feet up on my desk.

He pretended not to notice me for a few seconds, then looked up from his reading and said, "You know, Matty,

71

if this TV stuff ever palls on you, you could make a pretty good living as a blackmailer."

"Right," I said. "And when police work loses its magic, you can become a burglar."

"I don't know what you're talking about, boy. The drawer was open."

"I believe you," I said. "I believed Nixon, too. May I have my desk back, please?"

He got up and walked around to a chair facing the desk.

"The reason I'm here, Matty," he said, "is because we have come to that point in the investigation where we go back to the beginning. Mostly because we're not getting anywhere to the end. I want to hear your whole story again."

"You won't have to," I said. "Where's Rivetz?"

"He's looking into something interesting we found out."

"Too bad," I said. "I wanted him to hear this." I cleared my throat for effect. "I know who killed Carlson," I declared.

There was no expression on the lieutenant's face, but his eyes were bright. He said, "I'm waiting, Matty."

"Vern Devlin," I said.

He laughed in my face. That wasn't supposed to happen. He was supposed to be bewildered until I explained it to him. I don't think he reads the right books.

I waited patiently for him to stop. Finally, he mastered himself enough to say, "Okay, mastermind, Devlin killed Carlson. Why?"

I had been kind of hoping he could tell me. "I don't know," I said.

"How do you explain his alibi, which, I remind you, is supplied by *you*, along with an NYPD homicide detective and—"

"That's just it!" I broke in. "Look, when I was on the phone with Devlin, he wouldn't let me hang up. He was begging me to keep his name out of it. Then the two uniforms bust in and yell 'Police' loud enough to give every pimp in Times Square a heart attack. He *had* to have heard it. So, after begging me to keep him a secret, does he hang up the phone on his end? No. He waits patiently for Rivetz to pick up that phone and talks to him.

"He wasn't really trying to keep his name out, he was *stalling* me."

"Maybe he didn't think he had you sold on keeping
72

quiet, and figured it would be better to talk to the police after all," said Lieutenant Martin.

I thought about that one for a second. "How did he even know the police were coming? *I* didn't call them. Was there a vice raid in the hotel or something? Why were you guys there in the first place?"

"Got an anonymous call," he admitted.

"Aha!" I said. I was really into it, now. "Don't you see? Devlin made the anonymous call. He sneaks into the hotel by the back stairs, kills Carlson, sneaks out the same way. He calls in the anonymous tip, and watches for the cops to show up, all from the phone booth nearby. He's got some hooker or something handy, to fake the operator's voice, and times the call for when he figures the police should just be reaching the room.

"But, having sneaked in and out, he doesn't know the elevator's not working. When I wake up from the conk on the head he's given me, and answer the phone, he gives me the first phony story he can think of to keep me on the line until he can get his alibi firmly established. If I hadn't blundered in on him the way I did, his slight miscue on the timing wouldn't have been as important."

I paused for breath. "What's wrong with that theory?" I wanted to know.

The lieutenant looked exasperated. "The only thing wrong with it is that—"

The intercom buzzed. I picked up the phone, waving a hand to stop Lieutenant Martin. I had Millie Heywood on the line.

"Have you heard anything from the phone company yet, Millie dear?"

"Yeah," she said. "I meant to call you, but you should see what the assholes down here have done to me now. I mean it—"

"Dammit, Millie, what did you find out?"

It had been so long since anybody had yelled at *her*, she was shocked into absolute docility.

"Okay, Matt, she said softly. "Don't get testy. Here it is. Phone company guy I talked to even double-checked it with the switchboard at the place."

Here it comes, I thought. A nice juicy piece of evidence to hand the lieutenant. Then, with luck, I could forget the whole mess.

Millie went on. "Phone company computerized billing

shows that a call went from that Washington, D.C., number to the Hotel Cameron in New York City at twelve minutes after eight Tuesday night, meaning yesterday."

My jaw fell open.

"Huh?" I said intelligently. "That's not possible!" I exclaimed.

"What's the matter?" Millie asked. "Don't you like twelve minutes after eight? Anyway, the switchboard log at Communications Research, Inc., says the same thing. Listen, Matt, the guy at the phone company asked me why was it I was checking on the same call the police had been asking about. I'm not going to get in trouble, am I, Cobb?"

I couldn't stand it. "No, no trouble, Millie. Thanks a lot."

"Any time," she said.

After she hung up, I sat there with the phone in my hand, tempted to bounce it off the skull of Detective Lieutenant Cornelius U. Martin, Jr. He was laughing twice as hard as before. It went on a long time. A more embarrassed man than I was at that moment has never walked the earth.

Finally, he wiped his eyes, sighed, and said, "Matty, you've done an old man good, I swear. If you could have seen your face. That was the news about Devlin's call, right?"

I didn't trust myself to do anything but nod.

"I hate to be laughing at you, but it serves you right. You're a smart boy, Matty, and I'm the first to admit you've helped me lots of times. But this is murder, and you've got to learn you can't go off half-cocked. A report on that was on my desk before you were even brought to the office. *And* I had the D.C. police check it out at the source. The switchboard girl at CRI swears the call came from that building and that it was Devlin who made it.

"Now, let me have your story again. From the top."

I gave it to him, still saving Walter Schick. I was back in the mess, and I figured I *had* to solve it, in self-defense.

That point was brought forcefully home to me when, after I finished, the lieutenant said, "Okay, Matty, I guess you know what you're doing." He shrugged. "By the way, Tony Groat, the Teobaldi woman's boyfriend, is out of it —left-handed. There goes a top suspect."

"Who's the top suspect now?" I asked.

"If I had to name one, Matty," he said, "it would have

74

to be you." He picked up his hat. "Don't worry. I won't tell Rivetz about this afternoon." He walked out.

Back to square one. I might as well have been back in room 414. I opened a roll of butter-rum Life Savers, put two in my mouth. I went downstairs to talk to Jack Hansen.

Seniority, and the necessity of maintaining some degree of secrecy at times, got Jack Hansen's desk moved out of the directed insanity of the Channel 10 newsroom and into a little windowless cubicle that had been a broom closet in the original blueprints. He was editing copy for a public affairs documentary when I walked in.

He addressed my demeanor and general appearance. "Well, well," he said. "A midnight bender? You look like an unclaimed body."

"Considering how I feel," I said, "that's a compliment. I got your message. Got anything?"

"Quite a bit," he said. "Sit down. No, over here. I want a good look at your face while I talk to you."

"You too, huh?"

"What?"

I told him never mind. He put a briefcase on his desk, opened it, took out some notes. He was very professional. If the Network were to produce a series called "Jack Hansen, Crime Reporter," they wouldn't even consider hiring Jack to play himself because he looks too much like an actor; tall and slim, with his brown hair showing some distinguished-looking grey at the temples, and just enough worry lines in his handsome face to give it character.

"The first thing I found out is who found the body," he said.

"And?" I wasn't surprised. He had too many friends on the force not to have uncovered that.

"And you're lucky to still be walking around loose. That statement you signed looks like an excursion ticket to Sing Sing."

"That's the big story I promised you," I said. "A first-person account of how I did it." Seriously, I added, "Is that little fact important enough to use?"

"Not until they arrest you," he said. "Come on, Matt, you were a newsman before you went astray. This just isn't much of a story. Do you know how many bodies are found in hotel rooms in this city every day? If you want coverage, it's got to be the mutilated corpse of a little kid or something.

"I'll tell you what. I won't use the story until one of the papers or another station breaks it."

"Thanks. Did you find out anything about Carlson?"

"Yes, but I want to save that for last. Would you like to know the current thinking of the police?"

"I certainly would," I said. As the number one suspect, I figured I owed it to myself to find out.

Jack rubbed an eyebrow. "I got a lot of this from a certain file clerk who likes to peek at reports. I confirmed most of it with guys on the investigation."

He flipped his notebook open. "Okay. Carlson, under the name of Charles Vincent, checked into the Hotel Cameron at five o'clock. The day clerk says he had no visitors, as far as he knew, and the night clerk, that fellow who looks like a snap-bead, said he had one. You. That doesn't mean anything, though, because with outside fire escapes and the back stairs, the Detroit Lions could get in and out of the place unseen.

"Medical Examiner says death occurred at eight o'clock, give or take a couple of minutes, as a result of a piercing of the left ventricle of the heart. Death was practically instantaneous. The murder weapon was determined to be a knife, blade fourteen-point-six centimeters . . ."

"I saw the murder weapon. It was still in the victim's back at the time."

"Mmm hmm. Then you know the knife's of no big assistance either. In fifteen minutes, with just the money in my pocket, I could buy the identical knife, down to the pearl handle, from ten different sources within a block and a half of that hotel."

"You could have bought one in Moose Jaw, Saskatchewan, and brought it with you, too."

"Exactly. Worthless as a clue. Anyway, the blow was delivered overhand, from behind, with the right hand."

Explaining why Tony was out of it, I thought.

"Okay," I said. "I knew his ex-wife, I found the body, and I'm right-handed. I've known people who've been arrested on less than that. They haven't even had me down for questioning."

"Not everybody has saved a homicide lieutenant's son from drowning," Jack said.

"How do you know about that?" I asked.

"I checked up on you, too. I wanted a story ready in case you got busted." He smiled and went on. "Actually, I was kidding before. I know why you're loose. There are a lot of things they have to explain before they're ready to get rough on you. Or even impolite."

"Such as?"

"Such as the cigarette butts they found in one of the wastebaskets. They've been asking all your acquaintances if they've ever seen you smoke a cigarette. They even asked me. By now, they should be satisfied you're the worst enemy the tobacco industry has, outside the Cancer Society.

"Anyway, they're sure the cigarettes were smoked by two different people, even though they were all Carlson's brand. Some were left long, others smoked right down to the filter."

Now I knew why Rivetz and Lieutenant Martin had made a point of smoking last night.

"Hold it," I said. "The killer and Carlson knew each other, that's obvious. And they must have been there a long time, to smoke that many. The clerk can testify I got there only about fifteen minutes before the cops did."

Jack shook his head. "You could have sneaked back around to the lobby to make a phony alibi for yourself.

"And you're right saying it must have been the killer with him. It wasn't a hooker, no lipstick on the butts."

"Women don't all wear lipstick anymore," I protested.

"Hookers still do. And they don't take time for cigarette breaks. At least not the ones who frequent the Hotel Cameron."

"All right," I said. "That's one reason I might possibly be innocent. Why else?"

"Fingerprints," he said.

"Bull. That place has got to be *lousy* with my fingerprints."

"Sure," he conceded. "You left dandy prints on the doorknob, inside and out, on the desk, and the telephone. But there were no prints on the knife."

"I could have wiped it," I said.

"Sure," he said again, "but yours were the only prints in that room, except for the ones on the ends of the dead man's fingers. The ashtray that beaned you was clean."

"Then I walked in on the bastard just as he was finishing up wiping the place. He conked me and took off."

He nodded. "So, add the fingerprints and the butts to the conk on your head (sure you could have done it yourself, but why?) *and* the fact that the cops got an anonymous tip

77

from a man just about two minutes after you stumbled into that room, and there's a lot to give the DA pause before he's ready to try you for murder."

I felt a whole lot better. "Well, Jack, all I can say is thanks. But if I'm in such great shape, why are you so worried about me?"

Because he did look worried. He eyed me pessimistically and said, "Wait until I tell you about the victim."

"Okay," I said. "Let's save some time. He was a gambler."

"And a drinker."

"And a compulsive talker."

"Right."

"A loser."

"Almost always."

"Cards?"

"And horses."

"He was in a hole."

"When he died? Not too bad, a couple of grand. He had a good job at CRI. He was one of the developers of the overnight ratings, you know. Good pay, divorced with no kids or alimony (but you know that), he was in pretty good shape, for him. In fact, he made a payment to his juice man on Monday, probably one of the reasons he was in New York."

"What's so scary about that?" I wanted to know.

"I'm not finished. About a year ago, according to the word I get on the street, Carlson was down about nineteen grand."

I winced. I have pangs over plunging for a dollar for a State Lottery ticket.

"He paid it back, miraculously enough," Jack said. "Nobody is sure where he got the money."

"Wait a minute," I said. "You got this from your regular stoolies? Here in town? I would have thought he'd go to the bookies in D.C."

"This is the scary part," Hansen said. "Sure he went to the local boys, but after he started missing payments, the D.C. guys sold him to Herschel Goldfarb."

I didn't quake with fear. I did laugh. "Herschel Goldfarb?" I managed to get out.

Jack wasn't laughing. "I was afraid of this," he said. "Matt, listen to me. I don't know what you're up to, but you don't either, not if you can laugh at that."

78

"I'm sorry. But here I am, ready for a plot for world domination, or something, and you give me 'Herschel Goldfarb.'"

"Shut up and listen," he snapped. " 'Herschel Goldfarb' is not any funnier than 'Dutch Schultz,' or 'Meyer Lansky.' Matt, Goldfarb is a genius, possibly crazy. He could buy Central Park and put up condominiums on it, but he lives with his mother in a brownstone in the old neighborhood."

"Sounds like a nice guy."

"Keep it up, Matt, you can be the funniest guy in the morgue."

He rubbed his nose. "You know, Matt, a guy doesn't have to have a scar on his face and run around robbing banks to be a gangster. Goldfarb is a good case in point. Until about ten years ago, he was a professor at the Wharton School, an expert at management techniques and accounting practices.

"What he's done is to bring that expertise to organized crime. He's sold most of them on the idea of improved cash flow and lower overhead. He buys paper from bookies and loan sharks, getting maybe a twenty to thirty percent discount.

"Brilliant. They do it in legitimate business all the time. The way Goldfarb has it set up, the loan sharks have more money sooner (to put back on the street, or perhaps finance a dope deal), and are also spared the trouble and expense of collecting it.

"Goldfarb is happy, too. He can work on a larger scale than most loan sharks, so he has a very hefty sum of money coming in weekly."

"I'm sorry I laughed," I said. "I assume he's got a string of legitimate businesses to launder the money."

"Exactly. And he's a diplomat, too. He's very unobtrusive. Doesn't make the Family nervous, never jumps a claim or deals in dope, protection, or vice. Farms out the messy collections to soldiers in the Family. Keeps a small staff, two second-raters for driving and bodyguarding."

"And officially?"

"Not even for jaywalking. IRS has been dying to nail him for tax evasion, but he's his own accountant, and he's a genius; files every year, but the money's spread out into so many real businesses, and he knows so many loopholes, he never pays more than a couple of hundred in taxes every year.

"*This* is the person Carlson saw just before he got blown away. You watch your ass, Cobb, you still owe me ten bucks."

"I *paid* you during the Christmas party. I can't help it if you were drunk." It was a running dispute we had. "By the way, do the cops know anything about Goldfarb and Carlson?"

"Of course they do, jerk," he said. "They've probably got Carlson's movements traced back to the first one he left in his diaper. They're very good with that."

"Well, they were being coy with me then," I said, mostly to myself.

I thanked Jack, and left. In the hall, I pulled an about-face and walked right back in.

"Vern Devlin," I said.

He looked quizzical for a second, then said, "Rings a bell." He consulted his notes. "Here he is. Oh, right, that phone call. D.C. police talked to him this morning at CRI. Not much on him. Number two man to Carlson, probably will move up now. Bachelor, engaged, no money troubles that anybody knows about.

"Now, before you dash off again, is there anything else you want?"

"No, thanks," I said, and left again.

"When do I get my story?" he called after me.

I ignored him. I wondered when I would touch bottom with this case. I kept getting sucked in deeper and deeper. Now I had gangsters to deal with. What next, necrophiliacs?

I decided it was high time I brought my problems before a higher authority, and with God not posting office hours, I settled for Mr. Hewlen. When the elevator opened on the penthouse, the receptionist was somewhat at a loss, because I wasn't a senator, or an oil millionaire (foreign or domestic), or any of the other kinds of people that make up the general run of visitors to that office.

She was too well bred to goggle at me, but she was a second or two late with her superior smile.

"Matt Cobb, Special Projects," I told her. "I'd like to see Mr. Hewlen."

She was still smiling. With her pale complexion and wide red mouth, she managed to look not unattractively like a circus clown. "I'm sorry, Mr. Hewlen is in conference at the moment. Would you like me to make an appointment for you?"

"No, buzz him and tell him I'm here."

She let go a tolerant little laugh. "I'm afraid I can't do that."

"Sure you can. Tell him I twisted your arm. Or better yet, tell him I made indecent advances to you."

She gave a horrified gasp and buzzed. "Mr. Cobb wishes to see you, sir."

"What?" I heard the intercom say, "Cobb? Send him in, he's the only one missing."

I wondered what he meant by that until I pushed open the black leather swinging doors and walked in. I had a long way to look across the office, but even at this distance, I had no trouble recognizing Mr. Hewlen's conferees. The stern-faced man in the leather chair was Thomas Falzet, Network President. The red-faced woman looming over the Chairman of the Board was Cynthia Schick.

81

They each held position, playing statues while I crossed the office, down the five carpeted steps into the well that held the secretary's desk, up the seven carpeted steps to the level of Mr. Hewlen's desk.

When I was within hailing distance, Mr. Hewlen said, "Were you ears burning, Cobb?"

"I beg your pardon?"

"We've been talking about you. Why have you come upstairs?"

"I want to ask you a few questions. Mr. Falzet, too."

He smiled at me. I would rather see a shark dorsal in my bathtub than that smile.

"Well, answer one for me first. Why did you tell my daughter Tom Falzet tried to have her husband killed?"

Fate was throwing me nothing but screwballs. I slew Cynthia Schick with a look and said, "I said no such thing, Mr. Hewlen."

"You did too," she snapped. "You asked me if I thought Tom Falzet was so angry about 'Harbor Heights' and not being named President that he would try to have Walter killed!"

Falzet and Mr. Hewlen were regarding me intently.

"Well?" the lady demanded. "Do you deny it?"

"No," I said. "I asked you that."

"I *told* you, Father!"

Falzet spoke for the first time. "Ludicrous," he said.

"What is the meaning of this, Cobb?" the Founder demanded.

"I've been quoted out of context. I hope I'm not being out of line when I suggest your daughter is overwrought. What happened was, in connection with a matter Special Projects is looking into, I inquired about the circumstances of Mr. Schick's accident."

"He was murdered!" Mrs. Schick said, again burying her husband prematurely.

I didn't feel like arguing the point. "Whatever. Anyway, purely routinely, I asked if the police had ever suspected that everything about the accident wasn't kosher. She said no. Then I asked if her husband had any enemies, and *she* brought up Mr. Falzet's name.

"*Then* I asked her if she really believed he had done such a thing. She has probably neglected to tell you I went on to say *I* didn't believe it had been a murder attempt, because if it had, either Mrs. Schick or your granddaughter had to be an accomplice."

"You pig! Leave Roxanne out of this!" Her eyes were gleaming with hate.

I shrugged. "I would have, gladly. But if you go around saying I accused my boss of attempted murder, what am I supposed to do? Shut up and get fired? No thanks."

"Ludicrous," Falzet said again.

The Chairman of the Board said, "I apologize, Cobb." To his daughter he said, "Cynthia, I'm worried about you. I know you've suffered a lot during the last few months. We all have. I've allowed for a certain amount of stress and the effect it could have on your behavior. But I can't permit your emotional problems to cause dissension within the Network.

"Now, I'm going to have you driven home, and I want you to make an appointment to see a doctor about your nerves."

"I don't *need* a doctor, Father," she said, tight and dangerous.

The old man's face got as soft as I had ever seen it. "All right, Cynthia. Perhaps we can talk about it tomorrow. Maybe you'd like to go on a cruise, show Roxanne the world."

"Walter needs me," she said. We let that one float around the room a while and settle to the floor. By then, she was back to being her cool, efficient self. That woman was resilient, but you can only bounce back so many times. Finally, she agreed to discuss matters with her father later on. Looking daggers at Falzet, she left the room.

I looked around at the Modiglianis on Mr. Hewlen's wall while she was going. They all looked like girl basketball players.

After the door clicked shut, Falzet, said, "Ludicrous," shaking his head. "Well, Mr. Hewlen," he said rising, "that's that. I do think you should insist on that doctor. Now, if you'll excuse me . . ."

"Just a minute, please, Mr. Falzet," I said. "As long as you're here, I'd like to get my questions in."

He let me have it with his cold grey eyes. I survived. "Not now, Cobb. Who do you think you are? Make an appointment to see me in my office."

I was polite. "It would be a lot easier on me if you'd give me a few minutes now, Mr. Falzet."

"I've got an FCC commissioner waiting for me, Cobb. I could care less about making it easy for you." I winced. Saying "I could care less" when you mean "I *couldn't* care less" is like saying cold when you mean hot.

I didn't bother to reply to him, I was afraid he'd say something else to set my teeth on edge. Instead, I took out my wallet and removed a mimeographed message on a Network letterhead.

"Dated right after you became President of the Network, Mr. Falzet," I said. " '*To:* All Corporation Personnel. From: TJF. *Subject:* Department of Special Projetcs. It has been brought to my attention that certain individuals have been less than cooperative with (it should have been 'toward,' I corrected silently) the Department of Special Projects.' "

I nearly gagged over the next phrase, but I got it out. " 'At this point in time, I remind you that all Network personnel are required to cooperate fully with this department as regards information concerning the Network and its operations.

" 'Personal questions need not be answered, but failure to comply with DSP on any business matter shall be considered grounds for—' "

I had to stop. Mr. Hewlen was laughing his grey head off.

"Oh, Thomas," he wheezed. "You are such a pompous ass, you and your memos. Isn't he, Cobb?"

Should I contradict the Chairman of the Board, or call the President an ass? I ducked the question. "Alexandre Dumas the Elder wrote, 'One should be careful of what one writes, and to whom one gives it,' " I lied. It sent Mr. Hewlen off on another wave of laughter, and of course Falzet and I had to join in.

Falzet knew what side the butter was on. He put a good-old-boy smile on his face and said, "All right, Cobb. As Shakespeare put it, 'Hoist by my own petard!' Ask away."

I was impressed in spite of myself. People quote Shakespeare all the time, but they rarely are aware of it, so it was doubly surprising to hear it from a man that habitually committed such mayhem on the English language, even if he did quote it wrong.

So I was less antagonistic when I said, "Just a simple question, Mr. Falzet. Were there any recriminations when 'Harbor Heights' was cancelled?"

Mr. Hewlen butted in. "That memo specifically exempts personal questions, Cobb." He was enjoying this.

"Yes, sir. I was asking Mr. Falzet if he noticed ill feeling on the part of anyone in the Network or the production company."

"Oh. In that case, all right. You may answer, Thomas," he said helpfully.

"Thank you, sir." Falzet was good at controlling his face. He still had the smile stuck on, but he didn't like it a tiny little bit. He turned to me. "No, Cobb, no recriminations. 'Harbor Heights' was my baby, and of course I was disappointed, but we could all see it was going nowhere, and had to be terminated."

"Whose decision was it to yank it?"

"Well, mine, though Mr. Hewlen, Mr. Schick, and I all consulted together, of course."

"So you pulled it after eight weeks."

"Yes. Actually, in fact, after the CRIs for the second week came in, and we saw that huge audience drop, I was ready to cancel it immediately. It was dragging down the whole night, and would have begun to cost us money on the rate card. Mr. Schick agreed, but Mr. Hewlen advised us to hang on another month."

The old man nodded. "This way, the hyenas couldn't say we didn't try. If it didn't kill us on Friday worse than it did on Sunday, we might have kept it for a full thirteen weeks, like in the old days."

That was the first time I ever heard anyone speak nostalgically about the "old days" of audience measurement. Sampling research is a strange and fascinating thing. A constantly rotating sample of twelve hundred TV homes represents, for rating purposes, the entire population of the United States. It's a scientifically valid sample, mathematically accurate to within a couple of percentage points, yet some people persist in scoffing at the results. Someone once advised people who don't believe the validity of sampling research: "Next time the doctor wants to make a blood test, don't let him take just that smear—make him take all of it."

Anyway, in the good old days (about four years ago) the ratings were collected by attaching a meter to the set. The meter ran continuously, and recorded, minute by minute, whether the set was on or off and what channel it was tuned to. At the end of the week, the recording cartridge was collected by CRI, or mailed to them by the viewer.

Then some genius looked at the problem again. He realized that to identify any given show, the only bits of information you needed were the time and the channel. You didn't have to know that for each and every minute Sunday afternoon the set was tuned to the football game on Channel 2. All you needed to know was when the viewer *started* watching it, and when he *stopped* watching it.

So he got together a bunch of guys (including Carlson, apparently) and hooked up a system that works like this.

Instead of the old minute-by-minute, you now have attached to the television set a device that consists basically of three things: a clock, a recorder, and a telephone. When you turn on your set, the recorder takes down coded electronic signals indicating the time and the channel. Then it shuts itself off.

If you *change* the station, the recorder kicks to life long enough to make a note of the time and the new channel, then goes back to sleep. When you shut off the set, it records the time.

Now, you've got all this down in coded signals on magnetic tape. Then the telephone comes in. The other end of that telephone component is hooked into the CRI computer in D.C. At a preprogrammed time, the computer automatically places a call to your television set, and sends it a signal that causes it to play back all the information it's recorded. When the signal comes zipping down the line, the computer decodes it, adds it in with the info from all the other TVs, does the arithmetic, changes it into ink-on-paper so people can understand it, and *voilà!* ratings.

Now, the Network assesses its position not every two weeks, but every two *days*. And when the generals are getting fresh information, it gets hotter for the boys in the trenches. That's why the prime-time schedule seems at times to change while you blink. All the networks shuffle and reshuffle to get a bigger hunk of the several *billion* dollars spent on TV advertising annually. A tenth of a percent can be worth millions.

Falzet asked me, with polite sarcasm, if he could go.

"One more thing," I said. "Do you know an individual named Vincent Carlson who worked for CRI?"

"No. I have never dealt personally with CRI, though I will when it's time to renew the contract again. At this

Network, Cobb, the rating service is hired out of the budget of the Sales Department."

Of course, I knew that, as well as I know the color of my own eyes. But you never think about your eye color until somebody brings the subject up.

"Thank you, Mr. Falzet."

He went through the hearty chuckle, punch-on-the-arm routine again, to put the lie to the rumor that we couldn't get along.

Mr. Hewlen said, "Don't forget, Thomas, you and I are working late the rest of the week to discuss those pilots."

"Yes, sir." Falzet put the phony smile on again. "You know, Mr. Hewlen," he said, "I expect old Matt here is going to give us long and valuable service in Special Projects." He nodded. "He's different than McFeeley, but he gets the job done."

Different *from,* idiot, I thought savagely as Falzet made the trek out of the office. That bastard. He knew I wanted out of Special Projects and back into production. He had me low and tight. I could get a job at another network, but they'd only be interested in me for Special Projects work, or whatever they call it at the other networks. I could quit broadcasting altogether, but that would be like amputating from the shoulder for a hangnail.

When Falzet was gone, the old man speared me with a look and said, "All of that stays in this office, kid." He shook a bony finger. "Just forget about it."

"Forget what, sir?"

Evidently, that one was a regular thigh-slapper. When the laughter subsided, he said, "Cobb, I'm telling you this because I like you. Watch your ass. Your politeness is so obviously phony, it's like an insult. You're like me, can't appease people you don't respect. But *I'm* rich enough to get away with it.

"I know all about Tom Falzet. He's petty, and self-important, but he is one damn good executive. He won't let anything stand in the way of his own interests, but I make sure his interests run parallel to the Network's. He is a damn sight more valuable to it than *you* are, so don't antagonize him. Now what's on your mind?"

I told him the whole story to date, omitting only the current state of my relationship with Monica, and the details of my humiliation over the Devlin phone call matter.

He didn't bat an eye, not even when I told him about the

scene at Willowdale. When I told him about the attempt on my life, he could have been listening to a reading of the telephone book.

When I finished, he said, "You never told me this."

"What? I'm telling you now."

"No, you're not. You carried out the whole investigation on your own. You confided in no one else at the Network."

"Mr. Hewlen, somebody tried to kill me!"

He looked at me. For the first time since I'd known him, he looked old.

"Cobb," he said. "Don't you understand? I have built this Network. If what you say is true, or means something worse, *I must not be involved.* I'll be needed, to build it back up again.

"Cobb, believe me. No man ever lived who can say I broke my word. If any harm comes to you because of this, you'll be taken care of, I promise."

I snorted. "You mean you'll pay for my funeral?"

"Look. That was almost certainly an isolated incident. And even if it wasn't, it's probably too late, now."

"What do you mean?"

"The attack had to come because somebody sees you as a threat. How could you convince that person you are not? You don't even know who it *is.*"

He was right. The only thing I could do to neutralize any further night visitors was to go on and get to the bottom of everything, in spite of hell, if need be, or even Herschel Goldfarb. God, how I hoped his part of the story had ended when Carlson paid him the money.

The old man went on. "Come back here when you've found out enough so we can decide what to do."

I hated myself for it, but I agreed. His eyes had that introspective look old people often have; the look that means the person has decided that all the good parts of life lie in the past. It was new to Mr. Hewlen.

"I should have had a son, Cobb," he said. "Cynthia was always bright and ambitious and fascinated by the radio. When she was old enough to connect what I did with the programs she listened to, she looked at me with such pride and wonder . . . as if I were a magician or something.

"Did you know she's the one that thought of the name of 'Coony Island'? Came up with it when she was nine years old. Most successful kids' show of all time. Nine years old.

"Her mother died when she was born, you know. I was at an affiliates meeting in Chicago . . .

"Cynthia came home from school in Europe and asked me for a job. Said she'd do anything. I refused. Those days, only poor men's daughters had to work. That's the way it was, you trained your son to take over the business, and your daughter rode horses and played tennis. Today, things are different, I would let Cynthia have her career . . .

"She made a career out of Walker Schick. She channeled Walter Schick's life, Cobb. She made him make himself a top-notch executive. Gave him her backbone, or he would have gone all to hell when that fool daughter of his ran off. Walter always had the talent, but it was Cynthia had the drive."

It wasn't like he was telling me. It was more like he was dictating notes for his autobiography, and I was a stenographer. Just as I'd been for his daughter, I was an excuse to say in words what he'd been thinking a long time. A tape recorder would have served as well.

"She was always pushing me to name him to the presidency, telling me to step aside, that I'd 'earned a rest' was how she put it. But how could I step down? How could I? True, I own the biggest block of stock, but it's far from a controlling interest. The stockholders couldn't be expected to believe I'd named Schick solely because of his qualifications, and not because he was my son-in-law, could they?"

" 'Harbor Heights,' " I said.

I should have kept my mouth shut. He started to nod, but in the middle of it the spell broke, and he came to himself with a start. "All right, Cobb, you've wasted enough of my time here. I won't take it from McFeeley, and I certainly won't take it from you. Get out."

Quietly I said, "Yes, sir," and left him supporting his head with gnarled hands.

> *"The armadillo has natural protection, but you do not. That's why you should protect yourself with health insurance from Mutual of Omaha."*
>
> —Marlin Perkins, Mutual of Omaha's "Wild Kingdom" (NBC)

12

When I got back to my own office, I saw something I never thought I would: Detective Rivetz with a smile on his face. He was flirting with Jazz, and she was flirting back, just to keep in practice.

"Hello, Rivetz," I said. "What's new?" I figured he'd come around to give me the horselaugh for my blunder, and I wanted to get it over with as soon as possible.

The smile vanished. "All sorts of things, Cobb. I found something interesting just now, thought I'd ask you about it."

"Sure," I said, "why not? Just a second." It was practically five o'clock, so I told Jazz she could go home.

"Oh, thank you, Mr. Cobb." She was so enthusiastic, she had to be looking forward to a heavy date.

I invited Rivetz into the office. I sat at the desk. "Want a jelly bean?" I asked.

He turned me down. Maybe he had scruples about taking jelly beans from people he was looking forward to arresting. He said, "It's only a matter of time, you know, Cobb."

"Hold it," I said. "Hold it just a damn minute. Earlier today, Lieutenant Martin was here, all sad and sympathetic. Now you come around with the veiled threats. Are you trying a Beauty-and-the-Beast routine on me? Because it's not going to work, I know too much about it."

He looked at me the way I might look at a boll weevil, with a combination of academic interest at something I'd never seen before and disgust at what I knew to be a destructive pest.

"No," he said. "It's just working out that way, Cobb. The lieutenant *is* sorry for you. He's a good cop, even for a—he's a good cop, but he's known you for a long time, and he can't get himself to believe you killed Carlson for that Teobaldi twist."

"But you can."

"You're damn right I can, and I'm gonna prove it so even Martin has to believe it. After that, a jury should be no trouble."

"You had some questions?" I reminded him.

"Yeah. You know, this Carlson was in town *Monday*, a whole day before he called you. If he had something so important to talk about, why did he wait?"

I knew what he was leading up to. I figured I'd make it easier for him. "Maybe he had somebody to see," I said.

"Yeah, maybe." Rivetz was very good at looking cynical. "You ever hear of Herschel Goldfarb?"

"I've heard the name," I admitted. I didn't tell him it was only about an hour and a half ago.

"He's a crook, a money-hungry piece of shit. Carlson went to see him Monday, paid him fifteen hundred dollars on a forty-five-hundred-dollar debt. Guys down in D.C. say Carlson sold his car."

"So?" I asked. He was obviously waiting.

"So a while back, Carlson owed Goldfarb nineteen grand, which he paid back. Where did he get that?"

"That is the big question," I said. My being calm seemed to get on his nerves.

"You wanna know how I answer it, Cobb?" His face was red, and getting redder by the minute. "I say he got the money from his wife. I say he's got something on her, and he blackmailed her for that nineteen grand."

"You've got an exaggerated idea of how much money an actress makes," I said.

It didn't impress him. "She could get it. Woman who looks like that can always get it. But Carlson was starting back into the hole. He tried to hit her up again, but she wouldn't go for it, that's why he had to sell the car.

"So I say she looked you up again, lifted the skirt for you, got you to bump Carlson off before he spilled it."

"Spilled what?" I exploded. "Don't you read the papers? An entertainer can't be disgraced anymore! Illegitimate kids, drug addiction, homosexuality—Christ! You can't pick up a paper anymore without finding a story about some big star that not only does stuff like that, but is even *proud* of it. So what could it be, Rivetz? What's the deep dark secret?"

"We're working on it. Whatever it is, it's bad enough for Miss Teobaldi to skip out over."

"What!" I demanded. "What the hell are you talking about?"

He laughed. I was getting tired of cops laughing at me.

"So you really didn't know," he said. "You poor schlemiel. She's skipped, all right. Didn't show up at work, isn't in her apartment, isn't anywhere around. A neighbor saw her leave her apartment this morning in a real hurry with no luggage."

He laughed again. "She left you holding the bag. I could almost feel sorry for you."

I tried to think of a reason why Monica had run away, but the buzzing inside my head was too loud.

"But I don't," Rivetz said, "feel sorry for you. You bastard. You'll never know what you have to go through growing up as a Jew. People are too polite to say it, but you *know* what they believe. Even in New York. Even today.

"And some son of a bitch like Goldfarb comes along, and he's greedy, and he's shrewd—hell, he's fifty and he still lives with his mother even—and right away, that's all the evidence people need. Just one guy who suits the prejudice.

"So Carlson is blackmailing his wife to pay Goldfarb. Does she come to the police, so we can nail Carlson and use him to nail this bastard Goldfarb? No, she gets some idiot with his brain between his legs to do her dirty work for her, and Goldfarb stays home and makes plans to take his mother to Miami."

He'd had his voice raised. Now he lowered it to just above a whisper. "So now you know why, Cobb. I'll have to get as much pleasure slapping the cuffs on you as I would have slapping them on Goldfarb. Be seeing you."

It wasn't a friendly farewell, it was a promise.

First Mr. Hewlen, now Rivetz. This was a big day for getting to know people. Now I understood Rivetz. I didn't like him any better, but I understood him. Monica once told me her father used to sigh with relief every time he heard of the arrest of a racketeer who didn't have an Italian name.

Monica. What the hell was she up to? Where was she? I smote my psyche with those two questions all the way home.

Spot was frantic with joy to see me again. On top of everything else, I had pangs of guilt for leaving him locked up alone too much.

"Hey, Spot," I asked him, "how would you like a little kid to play with?"

"Woof!" he said eagerly.

"Okay, I'll buy you one. Boy or girl?"

"Woof!" he said.

"Fair enough. If I can find a woof, it's yours."

The conversation petered out, and my thoughts slid back to my interview with Rivetz. Should I have told him about my visitor with the gun last night?

No. Or Lieutenant Martin either. Rivetz's theory, as repulsive as I found it to be, was not nonsense. I couldn't prove anything about the attack. I could have bought that gun and fired a shot myself.

Okay. Welcome back, Walter Schick. I saved you for myself, and now I'm stuck with you. Back to basics.

First, a call to the Schick estate in Greenwich. I spoke to Agatha Locker. "And where were you on the night of the murder?" She assured me she was home that night, not choosing sides in an argument between Ms. Schick and Miss Roxanne about whether Roxanne should transfer to a college closer to home for the fall term.

"And what time was this, Mrs. Locker?"

"Oh, it started at suppertime and went on for a couple hours, at least."

"No one left the house, did she?"

"No, Mr. Cobb. They were fussin' the whole time."

"Thank you, Mrs. Locker." More good alibis.

"Oh, not at all. You know, Mr. Cobb, we have a weekly Bible reading around the various churches, and with you knowing the Bible so well, and having such a *nice* voice and all, why, you'd be welcome any time."

Poor sinner that I am, I was touched. "Thank you very much, Mrs. Locker. I don't know if I can ever make it, but I'm honored by the offer. Bye now."

I envied people who knew where to get their answers. All I ever seemed to come up with was harder questions.

I sat there feeling sorry for myself (something I do exceedingly well) until the doorbell rang. Now, that didn't necessarily mean anything, especially at that time of day. The doorman could have been hailing a cab for someone and a visitor was not called up, or it could have been one of my neighbors coming to borrow a cup of caviar or something. But after last night, I wasn't in the mood to take any chances.

I opened the safe, took out the gun Spot's playmate had dropped last night. Then I went to the door, and looked through the peephole. What I saw was a gigantic eye looking back at me.

"Who is it?" I demanded through the door.

"Tony Groat. Can I come it?"

"Back off the door, so I can get a look at you!" When he had complied, I recognized him as the kid who'd been in Monica's apartment the night before. He was dressed more conservatively today, with a buckskin jacket and dungarees. I put the gun in my pocket and opened the door.

"Don't do that anymore," I told him.

"Don't do what?"

"Put your eye up against the peephole like that. It scares people. What do you do that for, anyway?"

Redheads usually blush easily, and he was no exception. "I don't know," he said. "Must be something Freudian."

"Well, what do you want with me?"

He shuffled his feet and looked at the carpet. He looked younger than ever.

"I . . . I'm worried about Monica," he said.

I had to laugh. "Get in line," I told him.

"I mean it. I can't find her. Nobody seems to know where she is. She didn't come to the studio today, and it's an important episode we taped, too. Had to use a stand-in for Monica."

"Didn't she call in sick?"

"Nope. Nothing. This kind of thing could cost her that part in 'Deadline.' "

"What part?"

"Didn't she tell you? They're adding a female investigative reporter to the cast, and Monica is one of the actresses they're considering for the part."

"She didn't mention it. I was only there a little while."

He looked surprised. "Oh. I thought she might still be with you."

"The police are wondering where she is, too, Tony. A neighbor saw her zooming out of her apartment early this morning."

"Well, she hasn't come back."

94

"You've gone there already?" He nodded. "Did you go inside?"

"No."

"Why not? You've got a key, haven't you?"

He nodded again, blushing.

"What's the matter, Tony? You're acting like the teacher caught you hiding a hard-on under your math book. You were suave enough last night."

He laughed self-consciously. "I was pretty smooth at that, wasn't I? Shows what a good actor I am. What you got today is the country boy, not too long off the dairy farm."

"I've got you," I told him. "Been like a dream, right? Good job right away, beautiful older women? Don't worry about it, your ears will dry off in no time."

He perked up. "Happened to you too, huh?"

"In reverse," I told him. "I got out of high school just when this blue-blooded college upstate decided that the only thing it still needed was a winning basketball team. I was pretty good, and I had good grades, so they gave me a scholarship. After we'd won a few games, nobody could do enough for me. I had to check the mirror every morning to see if I was still me."

"That's it," Tony said. "That's exactly it. I keep thinking people are mistaking me for someone else all this good stuff is supposed to be happening to. I . . . I want to make sure it lasts."

"The best way to lose something is to want it too much," I said.

"Why do the police want to find Monica?"

"Well, one policeman, anyway." Now that I thought of it, Rivetz was probably heading for trouble, acting on his assumptions without consulting his superiors. It also occurred to me that here was a good way to ascertain how big his theories were going over with the brass.

"Look, Tony, I've got to walk the dog anyway. Let's walk up to her place and take a look around. Maybe she left a note for you or something."

"I just hope she's not hurt or sick or anything," he said. "Maybe she had a heart attack!"

"How old do you think she is, for Christ's sake?" I asked indignantly. "Knowing her, I wouldn't be surprised if she flew out to L.A. to try to personally convince the producer of that show."

We were both aware that was pretty implausible, but at least it got his mind off death and disease.

"Spot!" I called. The Samoyed trotted in from the kitchen. Tony made friends with him by scratching his throat, while I put the gun back in the safe.

"What a beautiful dog," Tony said. "Working dog, the best kind. We got a collie back home." He shifted the scratching to behind Spot's ear. Spot had his eyes closed, enjoying it. "How long have you had him?" Tony asked.

"Oh, he's not mine," I said. "We're just good friends."

I jingled the leash, and Spot came over to me. "We're going to give those hairy little legs a good stretch, boy," I said as I attached the leash to the silver-studded collar Jane Sloan had commissioned for him. She originally wanted diamonds, but Rick said no.

Spot gave me a facial. I will never understand how dogs get the idea that people think it's a treat to have their faces spread with dog spit.

Walking uptown, Tony told me all about his plans and hopes for the future. He reminded me so much of me, I wanted to tell him to go back to the farm and lead the simple life. I let it slide, because, if he *were* anything like me, he wouldn't listen anyway.

We made good time, pausing only occasionally for Spot to take care of the necessities of nature. In the gutter, of course. Spot was a very public-spirited dog.

Pets probably weren't allowed at Monica's building, but since there was no one to tell us so, Spot came along. I was glad to have him with me.

Tony used his key on the downstairs door, and again on Monica's apartment. It was twilight outside, but the rooms were dark.

He stepped inside. "Monica?" No answer.

I never actually thought so in words, but there was a formless dread in the back of my mind of finding another body. Spot was calm, though. I took it for a good sign. According to books and movies, dogs are supposed to bark or whimper when there's a corpse around.

There wasn't anything around, at least not anything that was at odds with the idea that Monica had left in the morning and just hadn't come back yet. The bed was unmade, and the pajama she'd worn last night was draped over the chair in front of the vanity. In the kitchen, we found a

used coffee cup in the sink, and a puddle of tepid water on the counter.

"Well, she meant to come home tonight," I said.

"Why do you say that?"

"Why'd she take the lamb chops out to thaw if she didn't intend to eat them?"

"Well, then, where is she?"

"Don't worry about it!" I told him. "She probably took the Circle Line tour or something." I was talking for my benefit as well as his. "Rivetz probably only made an issue of it to shake me up. He's got a mad-on about me."

Spot gave the kitchen a few tentative sniffs, then put his front paws on the counter and started scrabbling around. He looked as though he had evil designs on the lamb chops, so I pulled him out of the kitchen. Tony followed.

"Come on," I said. "We're not accomplishing anything here. If you want to come back to my place, I'll feed you, and we can talk some more."

He was willing. If he couldn't be with Monica, he wanted to talk about her. He was starting to get on my nerves, especially when he suggested calling the police.

"Look. Rivetz, at least, already knows she's not around. I don't know if he's saving it for himself, but if he is, and you call missing persons about a woman who lives alone being gone eleven hours, they're going to tell you to call back in a couple of days and that's it. If Rivetz has spread it around, the cops are looking for her anyway. If you want—"

I stopped talking because I caught a reflection in a store window of Shorty, my tail from the other night.

"What's the matter?" Tony wanted to know.

"Walk faster," I said.

We picked up the pace; our shadow did, too. We made a left turn down Broadway.

"What's the matter?" Tony asked again.

"We're being followed."

"That car?"

"Car?"

"Yeah, a green Ford. I've seen it three times since we left your apartment."

"Big blond guy driving?" I asked.

"I don't know," he said. "I'll take a look next time he comes by." He laughed. I couldn't see the humor.

Heading south on Broadway, we were approaching West

86th Street. That's a busy intersection, the kind where the pedestrian has to beat the "WALK" light, because the cars are all trying to beat the green.

Spot is a New Yorker, and took the lead in taking me across the street. Tony, not having been in Manhattan long enough, stopped at the curb.

Spot and I picked a path through the traffic when the light changed, the cars disappeared from around me, and I had the intersection all to myself.

Tony yelled for me to look out. I spun around to see a car running the red light, speeding across Broadway, heading straight for me. The tires were smoking, and the headlights seemed to get bigger and bigger as the car bore down on me, until they looked like two manholes to hell.

It was impossibly close. I couldn't jump out of the way. I was just hoping I could be dead before I felt the pain.

All of a sudden, I felt myself being propelled across the street. It was a combination of Spot pulling against the leash, which I still held tightly in my hand, and Tony tackling me from behind.

I hit the macadam and rolled, stopping only when I hit the curb. As my body rotated, I got a stroboscopic view of the green Ford speeding down 86th, toward the Hudson. And every glimpse I got, I got another digit of the license number: 297-VVJ.

My elbows and knees were banged up, and my hands and face stung where they'd scraped the road. I looked back across the street for Tony.

He was lying in the street, making whimpering noises and rolling from side to side. I ran back to him. The car had caught him as he pushed me out of the way. He was taking deep, rapid inhalations. His eyes were wide, and his skin warm and wet. He looked like he was going into shock. I took off my jacket and covered him as well as I could.

I wanted to get somebody to go for help, but the pedestrians had all mysteriously disappeared, while the cross-town traffic demurely circled us. They didn't want to get involved. I cursed them all.

Tony was trying to talk. "Legs . . . broke—"

"Shhh," I told him. "'Be quiet. I've got to—"

"Tried to . . . *kill* you." He had to force it out, but the sound of his surprise came through.

98

"I know, now shut up. Talking will only make it hurt worse. I've got to leave you for a second—"

He grabbed my hand. *"No!"*

"—only to call an ambulance. I'll be right back, I promise."

"Don't leave me!" he pleaded.

I couldn't waste time arguing with him. "Spot, watch!" I told the dog. That, I knew, would do it. Spot would stand next to Tony, and they'd have to shoot him to move him. A white dog standing there would lessen the chance of Tony's being hit again while he lay there.

There was a laundromat nearby with a pay phone inside. I called the operator, told her to get an ambulance and where to send it. Then, thanking God I'd remembered to take change off Buddha's lap, I bought a soda from a vending machine, dumped the contents in the sink, and filled the can with tepid water.

When I got back, the scene was the same as I had left it. Tony was still conscious, a good sign. Nobody was around. I wished Spot could talk, so he could tell me how many sons of bitches had driven or walked by without helping.

I went back to Tony, and made him drink some of the water, to ward off dehydration, which is one of the big dangers of shock. In small sips, he had put away about half the can when the ambulance arrived, along with a blue-and-white patrol car.

First things first. I told the ambulance attendant what I'd done. He told me it was good, and gave me my jacket back. Then I told them I'd been walking my dog and seen the hit-and-run. I described the car as well as I could, but I saved the license number for my own use.

I was mad now. At myself. Until now, I had been curious, depressed, but mostly scared. I had been breathtakingly incompetent in my handling of the case to date, but that had to come to a screeching halt. The good guys were starting to get hurt. The answers were going to be found, and *I* was the one who was going to find them. Starting now.

The first thing I needed was freedom of movement. I didn't know if my short friend had fingered me for the car, and I didn't know where he was now, but I wanted him off my ass, and I didn't want to spend the night at the precinct.

When the cop asked for my name, I told him "Lee DeForest," and made up an address. He didn't mention the scrape on my face. Evidently, it felt worse than it looked. He said detectives would get in touch with me. I smiled and said fine, and Spot and I got away from there, fast.

I was getting dangerous to be around, as Tony had found out. Unfortunately, I was stuck with me. I didn't want to be any more obvious than I had to be. That meant I had to get rid of Spot.

Easier said than done. Someone was stalking me, and I had to figure they'd staked out all the obvious places I could go: my apartment, Monica's place (no doubt picking up the trail of me and Tony at one of these), and the Tower of Babble.

I had to figure they were watching my parents' house as well, but even if they weren't, I didn't want to go there because Lieutenant Martin lived right next door.

I had to think of a place I'd never been before, yet where I'd be welcome. I could only come up with one possibility. I flagged a cab going by, and told the driver to take me to an address in the Bay Ridge section of Brooklyn.

"No way I'm going to Brooklyn, pal," he said. His breath was redolent of Sen-Sen.

"No?" I said. "The law says you've got to take me anywhere I want to go in the five boroughs, Nassau, and Westchester." I got in and put Spot on my lap.

"You wanna know what to do with the law, buddy? I ain't going all the way the hell over to Brooklyn. Sorry."

I gave Spot a little tap on the side of his muzzle. It's a little game we played called "Vicious Dog."

"Grrrrrr," Spot said.

"Gee, it's a shame," I said. "I've got to get there, fast. My dog needs his medicine."

Spot growled again, more menacingly this time.

"M-medicine?" the driver asked.

"Mmm-hmm." I nodded gravely. "Tranquilizers."

"T-tranquilizers?"

"Yup. Something wrong with his nose, you see. He thinks everything he smells is a cat."

I gave Spot another tap on the muzzle, and he really started looking ferocious, baring his fangs and saying, "GRRRRRR!"

The cabbie started to get nervous. "Well, I'm sorry, but . . . I mean, I gotta get rolling, you know?"

"Oh, I wouldn't dare try to move him now, the medicine

100

is nearly worn off." I comforted Spot, "There, there, Ripper, we'll have you feeling better in a jiffy."

"Ripper?" the cabbie gasped.

"Yes. Isn't that a cute name?"

Spot barked, and that was all it took. The driver said, "Bay Ridge, right!" threw the meter, and burned rubber out of there.

Spot calmed remarkably once we were on the way. The driver kept casting apprehensive little glances into the rearview mirror.

After getting lost only twice en route, the cab rolled to a stop in front of the right address, a dormered cottage, one of thousands of identical structures set six inches apart that lined both sides of the avenue as far as the eye could see.

Leaving the cab, Spot gave the driver's ear a playful lick. I suppressed laughter when he went white with fear. He probably thought it was a preliminary to having his head bitten off. He rocketed out of there as soon as I paid him.

Shirley Arnstein had the upstairs part of the house, one of those apartments with no straight walls. It had a separate door around on the side. I found it and rang the bell.

She opened the door as far as a magnesium-steel chain would allow, and said, "Mr. Cobb, what are you doing here?"

"Time to go to work, Shirley," I said. "Can I come in?"

The door let me see a tiny slice of her. She swiveled her head to look a question back up the stairs. A man's voice answered her. "Sure," it said, "why not?" Harris Brophy's voice.

With her glasses off, her hair down, and dressed casually, Shirley looked much more attractive than she usually did at the office. I was sorry for breaking in on her evening with Harris, and said so.

"That's all right, Matt. I can't resist her, either." His voice had its habitual tone of good-natured mockery. Harris was one of those supremely self-confident individuals. He seemed to be made up of equal portions of D'Artagnan and the Fonz. He had no arrogance in him, though, and was thoroughly likable. He was the only person I knew of who had turned down a promotion and gotten away with it.

"I'm glad you're here," I told him. "The first thing I wanted Shirley to do was find you. What I want—"

Shirley had to interrupt me to play hostess. "Mr. Cobb, can I get you something?"

"No," I said. "And call me Matt. It's a hell of a thing when the women in the department call me Mr. and the men call me Matt. First names from now on. And another thing. What time is it?"

Three watches came up simultaneously. It was nine-thirty.

"Okay, I want you to remind Jazz tomorrow to put it down on the time sheet for time and a half. You are now both officially on the job."

"Let me get my glasses," Shirley said.

"What's up, Matt?" Brophy said.

"It's important, but I don't want to go into the details. Briefly, I'm in trouble, and I need to stay loose until tomorrow morning."

Shirley returned, ready for business.

"I want three things from you two. Spot!" I'd had him waiting at the bottom of the stairs. He came up to the top and hung his muzzle shyly on the landing like a fuzzy-faced Kilroy.

"First, I want you to take care of my dog." They were going through the beautiful dog routine, and only half heard me. Spot came all the way up into the apartment, and pranced over to them instead of me, the fickle mutt. "Bring him into the office tomorrow."

"I'll take care of it," Shirley said.

"Second, I want to know about a green Ford Torino, New York State registration 297-VVJ. It was involved in a hit-and-run tonight. The police are interested in it too, but they don't have the license. The idea is to get Motor Vehicles to tell you what you want to know without it getting back to the cops."

"I know a secretary in the DMV," Brophy said. "It'll be a breeze."

"Good. If you can manage it, I want to know if that car is stolen, and if so, when."

With a confident nod, he said, "I know a secretary at Police Headquarters, too."

I would be hard pressed to think of a place where Harris Brophy *didn't* know a secretary who could tell him what he wanted to know. Shirley showed no reaction. She was being professional.

"Third, I want a check on the financial activities of Walter Schick from, oh, say June through November of last year. Thorough, but unobtrusive. That's for you, Shirley."

"Right, Matt," she said.

Brophy was intrigued. "Walter Schick? What are we doing, Matt? Hatching a plot to overthrow the Network?" He seemed delighted with the prospect.

"Harris, we just might," I said. I said good-bye to Shirley and Harris, patted Spot on the head, and went back into the night.

13

I probably could have stayed at Shirley's overnight, if I'd asked. Harris was whimsical enough not to have minded. However, I didn't think it was fair to take a chance of exposing them to whatever was after me. I was pretty sure I'd shaken my tail back in Manhattan, but I still wasn't sure what I was up against, or what resources they had. Though not petrified, I was apprehensive.

I wanted now to be within striking distance of Penn Station. I was going to keep my date with Devlin, and if he didn't come off that nine-thirty train, I'd go down to Washington and visit *him*. I had a new idea about the case, and I wanted to see what Devlin thought about it before I had cops laughing at me again. Carlson had told Devlin the assumed name he'd been using; maybe he'd trusted him with the big secret. Whatever it was, I hoped it wasn't what I was beginning to think it might be.

The first step was to get back to Manhattan. I no longer had Spot around to frighten cabbies across borough lines, so I headed for a subway station.

I descended metal stairs worn smooth and slippery by millions of pairs of commuters' feet, paid fifty cents for my token, and waited for a westbound train. I cursed the string of incompetent city administrations that caused the fare to be increased five hundred percent in my lifetime.

That way lay madness, I knew, so I took my mind off politics by reading the graffiti. The past several years have shown a new direction in artistic thrust of New York City graffiti; instead of the intellectually engaging (for example, "This Is Where Napoleon Took His Famous Bonaparte"), the movement has been toward the visually exciting. One budding da Vinci had used can after can of purple and

104

yellow spray paint to preserve the words "HECTOR 73" for posterity. Or, at least, until somebody painted over it.

There are few feelings as lonely as being the only person in a subway station. Your footsteps echo on the concrete platform, and the smell, compounded in equal parts of dust, machine oil, and sweat, makes you nostalgic for the noise and crowds of rush hour.

I walked away from the edge of the platform, close to the wall. I wanted to read the shy graffiti, the stuff you can't see in a darkened tunnel at sixty miles an hour.

That's where I saw it, written small between "Benny 102" and the curiously understated "carlotta loves raoul" in lower case. It felt as if the hand of Destiny had led me to that wall, even if I didn't believe in that kind of stuff. But it was so true, so *right,* it was like a mystical experience.

It had been written by a member of the old school, the graffitists who had more than their names and house numbers to share with the world.

I read it again.

"Help!" it said, *"the Paranoids are after me!"*

That was it, I realized. We're *all* paranoid. Worse than that, we're all paranoid, and we're all right about it. They *are* out to get us. Why? Because they think we're out to get *them.* And we are, so they won't get us first.

It had all the beautiful logic of madness. We run around, seeing everyone else as the agent of our destruction, so we take defensive measures that make us the agents of *their* destruction.

I pulled my mind up short when the train pulled in. I had a fifty-yard dash across the platform and a dive between closing doors to make it in. I always get in trouble when I start getting philosophical.

I left the subway system at Times Square, hoping to lose myself among the other homeless drifters. I walked around. I stopped in a steak house and ate. I got propositioned by four prostitutes, three of them female. I was exhausted and my head hurt. I had to get off my feet. The thought of the Hotel Cameron or a similar establishment didn't appeal to me. I figured the safest place to be would be alone in the dark, so I bought my way into an all-night porno movie.

It was a good choice. No bombs, no squealing tires, just violin music and groans to lull me to sleep.

The groaning was still going on when I woke up. "This is where I came in," I announced to no one in particular, and went back out on the street. I mixed in with the influx of early morning people, bought the morning papers, and settled down for breakfast at a pancake house.

I read the papers while I ate, finding nothing new on the Carlson murder, nothing at all, in fact. The story had backed right out of the paper.

At a drugstore, I bought one of those little travel shaving kits and a sewing kit. I ducked into a rest room, and, turning off my olfactory system, made my face and my clothes more presentable.

I had a lot of time to kill, so I passed up the subway and walked down to Penn Station. Penn Station used to be the same kind of monument to Victorian excess as Grand Central, but now it's just the train set Madison Square Garden keeps in the basement. Its concourse could pass for any enclosed suburban shopping mall.

The Arrivals/Departures board told me the Amtrak Devlin was supposed to be on hadn't come in yet. I took my *Times*, and retreated to a wall at a spot where I'd have a good view of the information booth. I was forecasting only a thirty percent chance of his showing up, but I wanted to see him first if he did.

I waited twenty minutes, but I didn't get a chance to get bored. In that time, I was invited to learn about four different religions, and was informed the world was coming to an end a week from Monday. I wondered why he bothered to go on the record with his prediction. Nobody would be around to give him credit for it.

I was explaining to an earnest young man with no hair on his head that I didn't *want* to bathe in the all-purifying Light because strong light makes me sneeze, when a man wearing a white carnation on the lapel of a charcoal grey suit appeared over by the information booth.

I looked at him in the barely adequate Light of the station. He was a little shorter than I was, six feet tall or so, with deepset eyes under an eyebrow that vaulted the bridge of his nose. He had paid twelve to twenty dollars for a haircut that had been designed to hide the movement of his hairline toward the top of his head. His features were unremarkable, but frowning the way he was, he looked mean.

He looked at his watch, scanned the now thinning crowd, looked at his watch again. When he raised his head, he was looking dead at me. He yelled my name across the concourse, and walked toward me.

"Sorry the train was late," he said, extending a hand.

I took it. If I regretted it later, I could always wash. "No problem," I lied, "I just got here myself."

He smiled. It made him look like a much nicer person. "Well, I'm glad I finally met you," he said.

"How did you recognize me? I was supposed to spot you."

"I found your picture in a back issue of *Broadcasting* magazine." He had shifted a small overnight bag to his left hand to shake. He shifted it back.

"Where to now?" he asked.

"My apartment," I told him. "We'll get a cab outside."

I decided to stop first at NetHQ, and told the driver of the cab we caught. Devlin and I were both silent for the first part of the ride. We were circling each other like a mongoose and a cobra, and neither one of us was sure which was which.

Devlin had a habit of, at about twenty-second intervals, patting his body gently with his right hand; touching his chest, his hips, his sides. It got on my nerves.

"What's the matter? Got an itch?"

"Huh? Oh, no, nothing like that. I think I lost my glasses on the train."

"You'll manage," I said curtly. "You recognized me from far enough away." I had a natural antipathy for Devlin, part of which had to do with his not going along with my theory. The spoiled brat part of me held it against him.

I wasn't about to let him out of my sight, so I told the cab to wait, and dragged Devlin upstairs to Special Projects with me.

Spot was making himself at home on the floor beside the receptionist's desk, making a game out of switching his tail out of the way whenever Jazz rolled her chair forward or backward.

I said hello to both of them, told Devlin to stay put, and whispered the magic words to Jazz that could make Spot prevent him from leaving. Then I got down to business.

"Brophy and Arnstein in yet?" I asked.

"Arnstein's here, but not Brophy, Mr. Cobb."

"Call me Matt," I said. "New rule I made up last night."

I reminded Devlin to stay where he was one more time, then went into Shirley's office.

"How did the dog behave?" I asked her.

"He was a real gentleman. By comparison with Harris, anyway."

"I don't want to hear it!" I said in mock horror. "Any word from Motor Vehicles?"

"No, it appears the secretary Harris knew has gotten married and retired. He says he has to start all over from scratch with a new one, and it might take a while before she'll do him that kind of favor."

"Great," I said. "How long?"

"He says he can't be sure, probably by tomorrow." It was typical; we both laughed. "He's a swine, isn't he?" Shirley asked.

"I don't know if it's better or worse that he really believes it. What's new on the Walter Schick finances?"

She eyed me curiously through her wire-framed glasses. "I wish I knew what this was all about." She shook her head.

"No you don't. What have you got?"

"Well, I can't say anything for sure, I've only given it a quick once-over; but so far, nothing. He drew his salary, clipped his coupons and the like. No expenditures out of the ordinary, at least during the period you specified."

"What did I say? June to November of last year?"

"Yes. Of course, I'll check everything over, but I don't expect to find anything more about Walter Schick. However . . ."

"Yes?"

"I only learned about it in passing . . ."

"Yes?"

"It probably doesn't even mean anything . . ."

One thing I've learned is that as infuriating as it may be, things get accomplished more quickly if you play along with the other person's dramatic pauses. It makes them feel better.

"Yes?" I said again.

"Walter Schick's daughter inherited some money."

I sniffed at that one for a second.

"How much?" I said.

"Fifty thousand dollars. It was left to her in her grandmother's will. That's the second Mrs. Hewlen, who died nine years ago. She left the money in trust for Roxanne Schick, to be collected on her eighteenth birthday, which was last July fifteenth."

"Saint Swithin's Day," I said.

"What?"

"Never mind, it just bubbled to the top of the tar pit. Do you know what Miss Schick did with the money?"

"Well, no, you did say *Walter* Schick. I could find out, but it would mean extorting from all those lawyers and banks all over again. What's wrong?"

From that last comment, I figured I looked as sick as I felt. I had hoped what Shirley had to tell me would dispel a certain idea I had that I didn't like. Instead, she had raised an even grimmer thought.

I sighed. "Well, don't bother about it yet. And don't refer to it as extortion. It's called 'collecting favors' around here."

"Semantics," she said. It sounded like a swear word.

"People like you are my crusade," I told her. I made her promise to read *Language in Thought and Action* by S. I. Hayakawa and have a talk with me before bad-mouthing semantics again.

I went back to the outer office. Devlin was still there, reading the bulletin board.

I figured my apartment would be safe this time of day. I brought Devlin there. I asked him if he wanted anything.

"Maybe a Scotch on the rocks to cut the dust," he said.

It figured he would be a Scotch drinker. Luckily for him, I had some, left over from a BYO party I'd thrown. I got him his drink, fixed something for myself, not Scotch. To me, Scotch tastes like Essence of Gauze.

He took a sip on his drink. "Nice place you've got here. That rug must have cost a lot." He indicated a white shag Jane Sloan had bought to go with the dog.

"Actually, it's not mine. I'm just keeping the place warm for a couple of friends."

"Lucky," he said, taking another sip.

"Yeah. It's my boyish good looks that do it." I took a sip on my drink, chocolate milk. I never take alcohol before sundown.

I decided it was time to get down to business.

"Why are you here?" I asked him.

"You brought me here."

"I mean, what are you doing in New York? Your name wasn't kept out of it. Why did you come to meet me?"

"Why are you so sure I came to meet you? Maybe I'm here on business."

109

"You wore a flower. I'm in no mood for games, Devlin. Why are you in New York?"

"I figured I owed it to you. After what the D.C. cops did to me, with my alibi, I could only imagine what you were going through, being found standing over the corpse and all. It wasn't your fault I was dragged into it."

"What did the cops do to you?" I strove to keep the skepticism I felt about his concern for me out of my voice.

"Well, they didn't beat me, or anything, but they grilled me for the better part of the morning. They got me just as I was getting home. I was tired, you know, I worked half the night."

"Even after you heard about your friend's death?"

"Look, ARGUS doesn't wait for anybody. Vince wasn't around, and I had to get that thing set up for the summer run. We do a lot of special stuff in the summer."

"How long did you know Carlson?" I asked.

"About five years. Ever since I started at CRI. He was my boss, but it's a small department. We got to be pretty good friends."

"How good?"

"Good enough to ... well, good enough."

"Good enough to know why he was killed?"

He looked surprised. "Sure, don't you?"

"I," I told him, "don't know a goddam thing, for sure."

He found that funny. "You know," he said, "when I got you on the telephone Tuesday night, I thought sure you had killed Vince to protect the Holy Name of Television. Or somebody like you had." He laughed some more. "So you don't know anything, huh? I was sure somebody would have figured it out by now."

"I guess I'm just stupid."

"I'll help you then. Vince needed money. Vince was in a unique position to control something somebody wanted to control. Vince got his money, but then he got killed."

I knew it. I had probably known it all along, but stifled the idea because I hated it.

Devlin said, "Ah, now you catch on."

"Spell it out for me anyway."

"If you want." He shrugged. "Vince was fixing the ratings."

14

So now it was out. I felt sick. If Devlin was telling the truth, Carlson had perpetrated the crime of the century. Or at least one of the top ten. As I mentioned before, *billions* of dollars are spent because of what the ratings say. To be able to add a point here, shave one there, would be the key to the strongbox.

You'd have to pick your spots, of course. It would be foolish to try to make it look as though "Meet the Press" had outrated the Superbowl, but you could cut the margin by enough to cause a lot of people a lot of trouble.

Worse than that, the industry's credibility would be blown. People trust the ratings. They may not like them, but they trust them. But once this got out . . .

Devlin grinned at my consternation. "Hey, look Cobb, don't take it so hard. Really, what's the big deal? My company does the ratings for your company so you know how much to rip off Madison Avenue for the opportunity to brainwash the suckers at home. What's the big deal if a guy decides to rip off the *first* link of the chain for a change?"

"Shut up. You knew about this?"

"Yes," he said, with an inflection that said, "what of it?"

"How long?"

He cocked his head to think. "Oh, since last fall sometime."

"When?"

"Let me think. Must have been Thanksgiving week. Yeah, because ARGUS was down, it was a black week, we weren't doing any ratings. Could I have a refill?"

I handed him the bottle. It had one of those valves on top that only pours a jigger at a time when you tilt the bottle. He tilted it a couple of times.

"How did you find out?" I asked.

"Well, like I said, the computer was down, and Vince and I were scheduled to do a routine check, but he had a tough night with the bottle the night before, and didn't come in on time.

"So I did it myself, or started to. I . . . how much do you know about computers?"

"Not much," I said.

"Oh, boy," he said. "This is gonna be kind of hard to explain."

"Well, give it a try."

"Okay. Right. I'll try it like this. A computer, electronically, is nothing but a switch, a huge, complicated, sophisticated switch, but still a switch.

"Now you take a light switch. It's either open or closed, juice or no juice, yes or no. Well, everything a computer does is based on a series of opens or closeds, signal or no signal. Got that so far?"

"So far."

"Well, that's it. There's room in the 'brain' of the computer for millions upon millions of signal–no signal combinations, with an unbelievable number of combinations. When we program the machine, all we're doing is setting up a series of these combinations to do what we want to do. I'm simplifying this a lot."

I told him I followed him. "But how did you find out he was messing with the ratings?"

"I'm coming to that. Now, for the convenience of *people* (ARGUS doesn't care) we break the kinds of information we put into the machine into categories, so when we want to check what's there, we have a label for groups of things. Like I said before, to the computer, it makes no difference at all, it's all still just a series of ons and offs.

"So what Vince did, was he hid a program to limit certain ratings."

"What do you mean, he 'hid' it?"

"Just that. He took a kind of information we call 'instruction' but disguised it as a kind we call 'data.' That's not all he did, but the rest is too complicated."

"How did he limit the ratings? I don't get that part of it."

"You know how the ratings work? Coded signals for channel and time?"

I nodded.

He picked up the bottle of Scotch. "Vince made a program that works exactly like this gizmo here. No matter how much booze is in the bottle, only a certain predetermined amount comes through into the glass.

"Vince set it up so the TV ratings system would only register a certain number of certain signals, and no more. It doesn't matter how many people are actually watching; the final printout will show what Vince set it to show."

"Carlson had this thing set to sabotage a certain show?"

"Right. After a certain point, it filtered the signal for that show right out of the system." He grinned. "Three guesses what show."

I didn't need them. " 'Harbor Heights,' " I said.

"Very good." He applauded me silently.

"No wonder the ratings got lower every week."

"No," he protested, "not at all. According to Vince, he only activated the computer program twice, the second and third weeks 'Harbor Heights' was on. He said TV ratings are self-fulfilling prophecies, he talked like that. He said that since ARGUS was implemented, shows are taken off the air so fast, that when the public hears a certain show has had bad ratings two weeks in a row, they stop watching it. Like rats deserting a sinking ship." He smiled again. "And the other outfits backed him up. *They* weren't fixed, but they showed 'Harbor Heights' taking a nosedive too."

I was holding in my fury. "And you let him get away with it."

"Hey, come on, he was my friend, you know? I asked him about it the next day, and he practically got on his knees to beg me not to tell about it. He said he hated himself for doing it, but he was in big trouble and had done it to get money to pay his gambling debts. He was a compulsive gambler."

"How does a compulsive gambler wind up in a position like that, for Christ's sake? Doesn't CRI check prospective employees?"

"Sure they do," he said. "But I understand Vince was a late bloomer as far as his vice was concerned. He was one of those no-sleep schoolboys at MIT. He probably never had leisure time to use up before he got the job at CRI. Besides, a lot of computer guys are fascinated with gambling, think they could figure it out, you know?"

"But not you."

"Not me. Five bucks on the trotters, maybe. I only like sure things."

"Okay," I told Devlin. "Now it's time for the big money question. Who paid Carlson to deep-six 'Harbor Heights'?"

"I don't know. Vince wouldn't tell me."

"Bullshit," I said.

He shrugged. "You don't have to believe me."

"I don't. I don't believe Carlson kept a secret this one time in his life, when I have it on good authority he had almost a compulsion to talk about his troubles, especially when he was pressed. And I don't believe you kept quiet about it without knowing the whole story."

"Sorry, Cobb, but I'm stuck with the truth. Vince was a good guy. He said he was keeping quiet to protect me. And I liked the guy, I felt sorry for him. Hell, his wife divorced him, but they were still making threats against her. It tore him up. He loved her until the end.

"Besides, it was no skin off *my* ass if some stupid TV show got cancelled a week or so early. I don't even *like* TV."

I stood up and pointed a finger at him. "All right," I said. "For now I'll take your word for it. But Carlson's conscience was getting to him. He was going to spill it to me, and he died. It's a good bet whoever paid him knows something about who killed him, if he didn't do it himself, and if you're holding out on me, and I find out about it, I'm going to personally hand you your head."

He raised his eyebrow, but didn't say anything. He pulled at his Scotch.

"I can sympathize with you, Cobb," he said. "When you find out which of the other networks did it, you can turn them every way but loose. They must have been real scared of 'Harbor Heights.'"

I doubted it. "Harbor Heights" had never been what you could call sure-fire stuff. If a rival network was out to do something bad to our schedule, why didn't they go after "The Jolleys," the top-rated show on TV?

No, add it all up, and Walter Schick was still the number one suspect . . . for the computer-tampering, not the murder. Ostensibly, Cynthia Schick had the same motive as her husband, but she had an alibi for Tuesday night. I could not believe the Bible-quoting Mrs. Agatha Locker had told me a direct lie. She might duck the question, but she wouldn't lie. Roxanne had come into enough money to pay Carlson, but why? Sure, she might have given or loaned it to her old man to use, but that brought us to the same dead end in the hospital bed for the murder. And Roxanne had the same alibi as her mother did. I wanted to scream.

Devlin was patting himself again.

"Will you cut that out?" I snapped. "It gets on my nerves!"

He grinned sheepishly. "Sorry," he said.

The phone rang. I jumped for it, hoping it was Monica. "Hello, Matt?" It was Cynthia Schick. I wondered what she was up to now.

"Hello," I said.

"Matt, I'm just calling to apologize for . . . for putting you on the spot with Father yesterday. I made such a fool of myself, I—"

"It's okay, Mrs. Schick," I said, "I'm sorry I had to say what I did."

"What choice did you have? I *was* a fool, I know. I just wanted to apologize. I . . . I want you to know I'm going to see that doctor. I can't go around losing control of myself like that."

I heard a noise behind me and whirled around. It was only Devlin opening the overnight bag, probably counting his socks, I thought. Your nerves are going, Cobb, I told myself.

I gave my attention back to the phone. "I'm sure he'll be able to help you," I said. "By the way, Roxanne didn't go to the movies in Bridgeport Tuesday night, did she?"

"No, Roxanne and I were both at home Tuesday, ah, talking. Why do you ask?"

"Oh, a friend of mine went, thought he saw Roxanne there. I told him he must have been mistaken. Listen, if I can do anything to help . . ."

"Just continue to be our friend, Matt."

"You can count on it."

"I knew I could. Roxanne sends her love. Bye, now."

"Bye."

I caught Devlin in the middle of a yawn.

"That was Mrs. Schick?" he asked. "Mrs. Walter Schick?" I told him it was.

"It's a shame when a beautiful woman like her has to suffer like that, I mean it."

"You mean it would be all right if she were ugly?"

He gave me a sly smile. "Well, you know how it is. Her husband brought her along for the big buildup CRI gave

115

for ARGUS, and at one of the banquets, I was at their table, to do the technical mumbo jumbo bit. I was charmed. That's a lot of woman there."

"You didn't make too big an impression on her," I said. "She doesn't remember you."

"That's a shame," he said. "Well, she's got a lot on her mind. A lot of woman, no man. Worse. She's got all the drawbacks of being married with none of the advantages."

"And you'd fix that."

"Not me, pal. My father taught me, 'Don't talk back to a cop, don't piss into the wind, and don't mess with married women.' Anyway, I'm about to get snagged myself."

The phone rang again.

I was more restrained about it this time. "Hello?"

"Good afternoon. Am I speaking with Matthew Cobb?"

"That's me."

"Well, Mr. Cobb, I'm calling on behalf of a Miss Monica Teobaldi."

"What do you mean, 'on behalf'?" I was irate. "Put her on the phone!"

"That's impossible, Mr. Cobb. Miss Teobaldi isn't feeling well. In fact, it's only recently she's recovered enough to tell us to get in touch with you."

Devlin said, "What's the matter, Cobb? You look sick."

I was sick. "Who is this?" I asked the phone.

"My name is Herschel Goldfarb," the voice said.

> *"Same to you, fella!"*
> —Bob Newhart,
> "The Bob Newhart Show" (CBS)

15

His voice had an amused undertone to it, like that of a guest at a funeral trying not to laugh when the minister's pants fell down.

"What do you want?" I asked.

"It's not what *I* want, Mr. Cobb. Miss Teobaldi wants very much to see you. She feels it will aid her recovery. Apparently, you have a beneficial effect on her health."

"Where is she?"

"In a very safe place, Mr. Cobb. I have an employee waiting in a car outside your building. He will take you directly to Miss Teobaldi."

"Do you know the penalty for kidnaping, Goldfarb?"

"Kidnaping? Don't talk nonsense. Some prankster lured Miss Teobaldi to my mother's address. She was taken ill, and Mother, dear soul that she is, agreed to take care of her."

So that was the way he was going to play it. The bastard could probably get away with it, too. If I called the cops in, he could fix it so that Monica just disappeared completely, that she had "wandered off in a daze" when no one was looking.

"Okay, Goldfarb," I said, "suppose I go along. Will the sight of me restore Monica sufficiently so I can take her home?"

His voice put on that chuckling tone again. It was offensive. "Well put, Mr. Cobb. Let me say I'm sure it will restore her to excellent health. She wants to see you *so* desperately."

"Yeah, I'll bet. See you soon."

He started to say something, but I hung up on him.

I turned to Devlin. "I have to go out for a while. You're welcome to stay here until I get back."

"Thanks, but that's not really—"

"Let me put it this way. You'd *better* stay here until I get back. Otherwise, I might start remembering things the police would like to know, not to mention the FCC. All right?"

"Well, since you put it that way, I accept. How long are you planning to be gone?"

"No telling. There's food in the refrigerator." That reminded me there was also a gun in the safe. I hesitated a moment, then decided not to take it out. I wasn't going to get anywhere trying to shoot it out with professional hoodlums.

I told Devlin not to spill Scotch on the rug, and left.

About ten feet to the left of the building entrance, a grey Imperial was parked. The driver honked, and I walked over and got in. There were two guys in the car.

"Where's your friggin' dog?" the driver wanted to know. He was big and blond, and one of his long arms had a bandage on it. The kind they put on when a dog bites you.

My brain sent a panicky signal to grab the door handle and get out, but before a muscle could even twitch, the sight of a forty-five caliber automatic cancelled the order.

It was my pal, Shorty, holding the forty-five. It was as big as his whole forearm. It looked like a howitzer.

"Relax," Shorty told me through his teeth. "Mr. Goldfarb only wants to have a little talk with you."

So he wasn't a cop. I forgave Lieutenant Martin.

"You'll forgive me if I seem a little dubious," I said. "I seem to recall Mighty Joe Young here coming to visit me the other night with a gun in his hand."

Mighty Joe started to sputter. "What? I only—that goddam dog! You made him attack me!" He showed me his bandage.

"Aw, poor baby," I cooed.

The jockey-sized one laughed. "It was just a misunderstanding, Mr. Cobb. Tolly was just going to invite you for a talk with the boss. You were just thrown by his approach."

"This is Tolly?" I asked, indicating the driver.

"That's him," the jockey replied.

"You got a name?" I wanted to know.

"Ray."

"Swell, Ray. You can call me Mr. Cobb. Do you people wave guns around the way other people talk with their hands, or what?" I pointed to the forty-five, which was getting bigger and uglier by the second.

Ray laughed again. It was a good laugh. He was the kind of charming son of a bitch James Cagney used to play in the old Warner Brothers gangster pictures.

"It's part of our job, Mr. Cobb," he explained politely. "We spend a lot of time *convincing* people. I've found that people listen better when you show them a gun." He stowed the cannon away. "Actually, this ain't got but one bullet in it. Tolly handles any shooting that might arise."

"So I noticed."

"Yeah," Tolly said, "and I want it back."

"Look," I told him, "you didn't show it to me, you shot it at me."

Tolly was a study in injured innocence. "I never would have took it out of my pocket, but you attacked me. I waited for you so I could ask you nice and private, and you opened that door, and that vicious mutt tried to bite my arm off!"

He eyed me suspiciously. "Did that mutt get his shots?"

"He's had his shots. And don't call him a mutt. He's got a better pedigree than you do."

I realized, to my astonishment, that I had fallen automatically into the cool private-eye routine these two seemed to be playing straight for. Maybe we had all seen the same movies when we were kids. I decided to keep it up; at least it was better than silence.

"Tell you what," I said. "From now on, you can refer to the dog as a 'son of a bitch.' That's accurate."

Tolly was puzzled. "If he's such a son of a bitch, why don't you get rid of him then? What's so funny, Ray?"

I got my next question in before Ray's laughter died down enough for him to explain.

"Who tried to run me over last night?"

Ray said, "Yeah, I saw that. How's your friend?"

"Are you trying to tell me it wasn't you two?"

"Are you crazy? Mr. Goldfarb wants to *talk* to you, he's a businessman, he wants to make a deal. You should have heard Tolly getting chewed out for firing a shot that might have hurt you."

"Yeah," Tolly put in. "That's another thing I owe your goddam dog."

"Now," Ray went on, "I know that wasn't an accident up there. Somebody don't like you, Cobb. All the more

119

reason for you to listen close to the boss. His friends tend not to get hurt."

We were in that part of Manhattan called the Lower East Side. Tolly pulled over to the curb. "Here we are," he said. "I gotta park the car. I'll be back in a couple of minutes."

"You're learning, Tolly. Keep the car off the street." Ray added an aside to me: "Lousy cops love to hang a ticket on the boss's car. Okay, Mr. Cobb, inside."

He was talking about a brownstone, three stories and a basement. It was in good shape, especially compared to the rest of the decaying neighborhood. It had flowers in the window boxes.

Ray kept me in front of him going up the nine stone steps to the door. I stood waiting at the top of the stoop until he caught up. He surprised me by ringing the bell instead of walking right in. I had just assumed that a henchman would walk right in.

I got another surprise when the door was opened by a sweet-looking little old lady in a purple housedress and orthopedic shoes.

"Oh, hello, Ray," she said. She gave him a little kiss on the cheek that made him squirm like an eight-year-old. "Herschel is in the study," she said.

She turned her smile on me. "And this must be Monica's boyfriend. Well, don't worry, I'm taking good care of her."

"I . . . uh . . . I can't tell you how much I appreciate it," I told her, truthfully.

She had a twinkle in her eye. "It's awful to say this, but I'm glad it happened. An old woman likes to meet young people. And maybe if Herschel sees how happy you two are, he'll get some ideas, hah? Don't get me wrong, my Herschel is a very good son, the best, but at his age . . ."

"Hey, Mrs. G.," Ray interrupted, "don't you think Mr. Cobb would like to see his girl?"

She clicked her tongue, chiding herself. "Of course, what's the matter with me, a silly old woman, talks too much. Go, go. I have to dust. You'll stay for dinner, won't you, Matt, I think your name is?"

"He'll be delighted to," Ray said. He hustled me off to the study, where I got my first look at Herschel Goldfarb.

It was the most frightening experience of my life. Not because Goldfarb was the incarnation of evil and corruption. Just the opposite. Herschel Goldfarb was a dead ringer for Ozzie Nelson.

It was obscene. Think of it: Ozzie Nelson, crewcut, crinkly eyes, mild tenor; the original Mr. Nice Guy, whose only occupation seemed to be arranging prom dates, suddenly reincarnated as a desperate criminal.

Well, maybe not desperate. Goldfarb, dressed in the Ozzie Nelson garb of sweater, white shirt and tie, slacks and slippers, was sitting calmly on the sofa reading the second edition of the *New York Post*.

"Glad you could come, Mr. Cobb," he said. It was weird to hear the deep voice and formal speech coming from that body. "Did you have a pleasant drive?"

"Positively divine," I told him. "Tolly taught me the multiplication tables." I had decided to stay with the light touch.

"Ah, Mr. Cobb, you mustn't judge the boy too harshly. Intelligent men tend to place too much value on intelligence."

"I don't know. I wouldn't be in this mess if I had any intelligence."

Goldfarb's chuckle was worse in person that it had been on the phone. "That's a good one," he said. "But I maintain intelligence isn't everything. Tolly is loyal, strong, and has a unique combination of sensitivity and brutality in his makeup."

"Like a Saint Bernard," I said.

"Exactly!" He beamed at me. "That's exactly it. Now, Ray, while not brilliant, is very shrewd, and knows his way around the sort of people I deal with in my business."

"*I* don't care if you keep them around to light the stove on Friday. I want to see Monica."

Just then, Tolly opened the double door (both sides) and walked in.

"Ah, Tolly, Mr. Cobb and I were just discussing how valuable your services are to me."

Tolly blushed.

"Tolly, go upstairs and tell Miss Teobaldi I'd like to see her in the study. If she's asleep, though, call my mother to awaken her. Do you understand?"

Tolly nodded, and backed out of the room, closing the doors after him.

"He has a tendency to touch women in embarrassing

121

places," Goldfarb confided. "Curiosity. In many ways, Tolly is like a child."

I surveyed the room while we waited. It was a comfortable-looking place, if a little out of fashion. Bookshelves lined three walls, filled with books in many languages. All the titles in the four languages I can read were concerned with economics.

The rest was very Victorian. Wingback chairs (with antimacassars) on a flowered rug. Ornate lamps and lamp tables, and knickknacks everywhere.

One side of the double door opened, and Monica stepped in. She was dressed for the street, in a silk blouse and corduroy skirt. She had stockings on, but no shoes. Her hair was a mess, and there were tear tracks on her face.

She saw me, cried, "Matt!" and ran toward me. Tolly and Ray both moved to stop her, but they froze on a syllable from Goldfarb.

Monica and I held each other tight. "Oh, Matt, I've been so afraid."

"Shhh," I said. "It's almost over now." That was probably true, I figured, one way or the other.

"How long have I been here?" she asked. "I've been unconscious."

"A little less than two days, babe." I looked to Goldfarb over her head. The bastard was smiling. "What has she been on? What did you dope her with?"

"Don't get so excited, Mr. Cobb. Miss Teobaldi seems better already, I knew your visit would do her good. Please rest assured she was given nothing stronger than scopolamine, which you can buy without prescription in many cold remedies. It was administered by a doctor."

"What happened?" I asked Monica.

"I don't know. I . . . I got a phone call this morning—"

"Wednesday morning," Goldfarb corrected good-naturedly.

"—somebody saying you'd been hurt and brought to the hospital. You didn't answer your phone, you weren't at your parents' house. I got to the hospital, and as I was crossing the lobby, I started to feel dizzy, and when I woke up, I was here."

"Somebody bumped into you and gave you an injection," I told her. "How do you feel?"

"I'm still pretty drowsy," she said. "Matt, I want to go home."

So did I. "All right, Goldfarb," I said. "Let's get down to business. What do you want from me?"

"Sit down, please, both of you. That's better. I'm sure we can settle this easily." He made the same smile Ozzie Nelson used to accompany an offer of cookies and milk. "Before I tell you what I expect of our . . . ah . . . association, I'm going to tell you about myself. I want you to know the sort of person you will be dealing with."

I couldn't resist. "With whom you will be dealing, you mean. You should never use a preposition to end a sentence with."

"Very amusing," he deadpanned. "Perhaps you made a mistake when you gave up your ambition to teach."

"I've often felt that way," I admitted.

"I was a teacher myself, as you probably know. Until ten years ago, I was a professor of economics. I am still one of the world's foremost experts in corporate accounting. My books are still used as texts at many colleges.

"But as my theories gained wider and wider acceptance, I became less and less happy. I saw the huge multinational corporations make unprecedented profits. I had made it possible for strangers, foreigners to make billions. Even the *Arabs* enriched themselves with *my* ideas.

"And I had nothing. Oh, I made a salary, a good one by most standards, but I had no *wealth*. Do you understand the difference between money and wealth, Mr. Cobb?"

"Money is the result of wealth," I told him. "A producing oil well is wealth. A factory. A diner where the food is good."

He beamed at me. "You would have been an excellent teacher. With all my degrees, I couldn't have defined it better. I would have thought, though, that you might have included a high-rated television show in your definition.

"So one day, I came to my senses. My mother was ill, desperately ill. She had to sell this house to raise money for treatment, even though I had helped her all I could.

"What kind of a son would allow that to happen? Not the kind my mother deserves. I vowed to make it up to her."

Goldfarb stood up, and began pacing back and forth, hands clenched behind his back, just the way he probably had when he lectured the grad students in Accounting 605.

"I would be the last to deny that one may legally acquire wealth," he went on, "even with the limited capital I had

123

at the time, but it takes too long, and I had already wasted enough time. I chose to work outside the law, and avoid such distractions as income tax, maximum interest rates, and antitrust laws. I took my capital, and using my theories to my *own* advantage, along with the . . . ah . . . uninhibited business practices customary outside the law, I have accumulated much money. And much wealth. I have bought this house back for my mother . . . and five others around the world."

"A veritable Napoleon of crime," I said.

He laughed. "Hardly a Moriarty, Mr. Cobb. I don't direct or control many criminal enterprises, I merely arrange things so I profit from them.

"And that brings me to the point, Mr. Cobb. I am angry with you. I've been polite and even friendly, but you have made me very angry."

"How the hell did I accomplish that?" I demanded. "I didn't even know you existed until yesterday."

"It wasn't necessary to know of my existence. You have done the one thing I will not tolerate. You have deprived me of a source of wealth."

Monica looked at him, then at me, then back to him, then back to me. "What is he talking about?" she asked.

"Damned if I know."

"Please spare me the coyness. You deprived me of a source of wealth with a potential return of millions of dollars when you murdered Vincent Carlson."

I shook my head, resigned. "Boy," I said, "once a rumor gets started . . . I suppose you know you're insane?"

"I beg to differ with you. A man is found with the body of a man he's never met, but who just *happens* to be the ex-husband of his former lover. Questioned by the police, then released, he makes straight for the apartment of the woman, where he spends over an hour. What is one supposed to think?"

"One thinks Goldfarb owns a cop," I said. "One thinks one was tailed."

He laughed. "Ray was waiting for you outside Police Headquarters, with instructions to follow you and bring you to me when you returned home. He failed, as you know. Tolly waited for you at your apartment. He also failed.

"In any event, you handled Tolly so easily—"

124

That was too much for Tolly. "It wasn't him, it was that son-of-a-bitch dog!"

"You know better than to interrupt me, Tolly." He said it calmly, but Tolly turned off the anger immediately. He looked sheepish, and seemed to get smaller as we watched.

"As I was saying. You were so resourceful, I decided to study you before we talked business."

"Yeah?" I said. "What kind of business did you have in mind with that car on 86th Street last night? What kind of study? Were you going to take a smear of me and do a microscopy?"

"Nonsense. It was someone else who tried to run you down. You seem to have a knack for offending people."

I didn't say anything, but for the first time, I was faintly encouraged. If it had been someone else and not Goldfarb, it meant Goldfarb didn't want me dead; at least not immediately. If it had been Tolly or Ray at the wheel, the fact that they were lying about it had to mean they cared what I thought, which meant I'd be around to think for a little while, anyway.

Monica looked concerned. "Somebody tried to kill you?" I had forgotten this was the first she was hearing about it, and the horrified look on her face surprised me.

"They tried, all right," I said. "Tony and Spot saved my life. Tony got a couple of broken legs out of it."

"Oh, my God," she said.

"Who is Tony?" Goldfarb demanded.

"Friend of ours," I replied.

"My deepest sympathy," he said sincerely. "I hope you both will be able to extend it to him. Now, to get back to our discussion. Under ordinary circumstances, having done what you did—"

I broke in. "Just for the record, I didn't do it. Most of the police don't think so either."

That amused him. "I know. This is the first time Detective Rivetz and I have agreed on anything. By the way, to correct your earlier misassumption, I *don't* own any policemen, and don't want to. The more people on your payroll, the more witnesses there may be to testify against you, remember that, Cobb. I get information secondhand, maybe thirdhand, but I always know what I need to know. I know what the police think.

"But the police are required to prove what they think, and I am not. I think you are intelligent enough to arrange the evidence to make it look unlikely you murdered Carlson. There was enough at stake."

Monica caught Goldfarb's crinkly eyes. "Matt was right, you know. You *are* crazy."

"All the worse for the two of you if I am," he said. He was furious. He no longer looked like Ozzie Nelson. Ozzie Nelson was never furious. "The only reason you haven't vanished without a trace, Mr. Cobb, is my suspicion that *you* may replace Mr. Carlson as a source of wealth."

I said nothing. It seemed to throw Goldfarb for a loss, as though the conversation had been scripted, and I'd missed my cue.

He struggled on. "Because you didn't kill Carlson solely from lust. You wouldn't, I know, having studied you. And Rivetz's blackmail theory is ludicrous. But Carlson, in order to pay his debt to me, had done something with as much earning potential as any development in this century. You killed him to get control of that development."

"How about letting me in on what I killed him to get?"

"As if you didn't know." Goldfarb was disappointed in me. "Carlson was a brilliant man, but he had a very loose mouth. It took very little pressure to get him to tell *me* what it was. Surely his wife was told. Surely, she told her lover."

He was truly insane. The wronger he got, the more positive he was.

"Humor me," I said.

"Very well. Carlson had developed a way to prearrange the ratings of any television program."

So. I was sorry Devlin had come by that morning, because I was better at telling the truth than I was at lying. Now I was stuck with lying.

"And you believed him?" I laughed derisively. "He was pulling your leg."

"I doubt it. Carlson feared me. He said he had done it once, and would never do it again. He didn't say exactly who paid him, and I didn't press him about that. As long as there were horses, I knew Vincent Carlson was mine. He would have done it again and again, as often as I told him to."

"Why?" I demanded. "What's in it for you?"

"Mr. Cobb, don't you see the possibilities? Of course you do. Why you maintain your pose is beyond me. But I will tell you anyway.

"Extortion, Mr. Cobb. Tell a struggling producer we can guarantee that his show will be a hit. Bribes. Many businessmen, legitimate or otherwise, have 'protégées' who like to think they are actresses or singers. We could assure these men their protégées would produce exceptionally high ratings whenever they appeared on television. Clairvoyance. We could place advertisements for products in which we own an interest on certain programs, and destroy the programs on which our competitors advertise.

"Of course, this is only off the top of my head. The possibilities are unlimited!" He swept his arms to indicate the scope of the possibilities. His face was aglow with enthusiasm.

"Uh huh," I said, "and what happens when people start to notice the discrepancies between CRI and everyone else?"

Goldfarb looked pleased. "You see? Your expertise is paying off already. I hadn't thought of that. We must take steps to avoid that for as long as possible."

"This is the royal 'we' you're using, I take it."

"Not at all, Mr. Cobb, not at all. I am referring to you and me. I intend to reward you handsomely. It's good business practice to pay a man what he is worth."

Monica made a little choking noise. She looked as though she were going into shock.

"You make it sound good," I told Goldfarb. "I wish I could help you."

"Of course you can help me."

I shook my head. "Nope. Sorry. I'm honest, I can't help it, it's a congenital defect." I rose. "Let's go, Monica."

One one-hundredth of my mind thought it might work, that Goldfarb would actually let us walk out that door; the rest was just interested in seeing how far we got.

I had my hand on the doorknob when Goldfarb spoke up.

"I believe you're forgetting something, Mr. Cobb."

I hadn't forgotten. I turned around to see Goldfarb's smiling face, and Tolly and Ray holding guns on us.

> *"A marvelous dish . . . just for you."*
> —Graham Kerr, "The Galloping
> Gourmet" (syndicated)

16

When we had returned to our chairs, Goldfarb said, "I expected better of you, Cobb." I noticed the "mister" was gone.

I shrugged.

"Surely you must realize that we've discussed the subject too deeply for either of you to leave here as anything but my partner."

"Or dead," Monica said quietly. It was kind of a question.

Goldfarb waved it off. "I'm sure we can come to an agreement. You've gone too far to stop now. I can understand your disappointment at having to share the fruits of your work, but murderers before you have been forced to take on . . . ah . . . partners. I sympathize with you. But there is too much money to be made using Carlson's process for me to stay away. You are going to tell me how to control the CRI ratings."

"Watch my lips," I said. "I didn't kill Carlson. I don't know how to fix the ratings. Got that?"

He shook his head. "Nonsense. You are in precisely the same position I was in ten years ago. Your work has made a mockery of you. Because of your excellence at a job you enjoyed, you have been forced to work at one you despise. It was inevitable that you would break out, grab something for yourself."

"You know, I can't figure out what it is about me," I said. "People have this almost irresistible urge to analyze me, and they're almost always wrong. Now, take you for instance. I—"

I never got to finish that sentence, which was just as well, since I was only talking to keep Goldfarb shut up for a while. What interrupted me was the door opening, and the sweet face of Mrs. Goldfarb poking in to announce that supper was ready.

It wasn't long before I found out another reason besides filial loyalty that Goldfarb had thrown over the college gig and come home. His mother was the best cook on the Eastern seaboard. There was probably never a time I felt less like eating, but by God, I put it away, roast beef with the smoothest gravy, stuffed derma, carrots and peas, home canned (I found out) and picked personally by Mrs. Goldfarb. For dessert, there was noodle pudding that was so good I had to wonder how anyone brought up by a mother who made it could turn out to be such a louse.

Monica ate sparingly, with her eyes down, and was clucked at accordingly by Mrs. Goldfarb.

I figured with his mother there, Goldfarb would have to at least let me talk. I stowed away a forkful of noodles and said, "So, Mr. Goldfarb, even assuming I have the basic knowledge to perform the job you've offered me, and I assure you again, I don't, certain recent developments have put me under some suspicion, and I wouldn't have the opportunity to *do* it. So I have to decline your offer, as much as I hate to." I was talking about being suspected of murder.

He understood me fine. Wiping his mouth, he said, "Mother, I'm so proud. You always seem to outdo yourself when I have guests.

"You underrate yourself, Mr. Cobb, and me. I have many friends. A word from me, and they would see to it that those ugly rumors stop. People can always be persuaded, if one goes about it the right way."

I was going to protest, but his mother cut me off. "You shouldn't bother to argue with him, Matt—I may call you Matt?"

"Sure," I said. Why not? I liked *her*.

"Thank you," she said primly. "No one can argue with my Herschel. Once he decides what he's going to do, you might as well argue with the walls. He's a very strong-minded boy."

Her Herschel was beaming. It occurred to me that that overgrown mama's boy wasn't as crazy as he acted, that he was just playing the percentages. The way he saw it, the possible return from rigging the ratings far outweighed the nuisance of possibly having to waste a couple of schnooks if they wouldn't or couldn't come across.

That made it worse. And even if I *did* tell him, I had the feeling Devlin would work his way into the picture and I would be superfluous. There was no guarantee Goldfarb wouldn't wipe us out just on general principles, even before he found Devlin.

It stank no matter what direction I sniffed it from. I knew I had to do something, but trying to take on two (or possibly three) armed men seemed a little drastic at the moment. I tabled that one for the Last Resort meeting.

Goldfarb wanted to talk some more. I decided I was going to string along with him, trying to buy some time. But just as we were getting settled back in the study, Mrs. Goldfarb poked her head in again. It must be tough being a criminal with your mother always hanging around.

"Herschel, darling," she said. "I have an appointment at the doctor this evening, I forgot all about it."

Her son was very solicitous. "I'm sorry to say I did, too. I'll call a taxi right away. Can you still be on time?"

"Yes, if I start right away, but . . . are you going to let your mother go alone? You know I don't like to go out alone at night. I don't want to take you away from your friends . . ."

"We don't mind," I said, being helpful.

Goldfarb was thinking it over. He looked appraisingly at Monica and me, then helplessly at his mother. Finally he said, "Of course I'll come with you, Mother. I've been meaning to have a chat with that doctor, anyway."

He turned to Ray. "Ray, I think we've talked enough business for one day. I think Mr. Cobb and Miss Teobaldi would enjoy seeing my mother's cottage at the beach."

"Oh, yes," Mrs. Goldfarb said. "My Herschel bought it for me. It's really beautiful."

"Perhaps they'd even like to stay the night there."

"Herschel!" his mother scolded, but her eyes were twinkling. I wondered again how a nice lady like that could produce such a creep.

"And Ray," Goldfarb said, "be sure to bring the things from the safe with you."

"Yes, sir."

"Be *very* careful with them."

"Yes, sir."

After an uncomfortable five minutes, with everyone standing around trying to be polite, a cab honked outside, and Goldfarb and his mother were off to the doctor's. After they had gone, Tolly began to laugh.

"What's so funny?" Monica asked him.

"The old lady thought—the boss—ha ha—she thought he was fixing you up so you two could ha ha ha." He sighed. "Ain't that cute?" He laughed again. Monica shuddered.

Ray, meanwhile, had unlocked a desk drawer and come out with two pairs of handcuffs. They were shinier than the ones I had seen the police carrying Tuesday night, but that was the only difference. Probably because cops use theirs more often.

"What are those for?" I asked.

"To make sure you stay in the car," Ray said matter-of-factly. "Coming in, you had reason to stay in the car, but now, you got reason to try to get out."

"What's that supposed to mean?"

"I like you, Cobb, you're what they call a likable guy, you know? But you're thickheaded. You're too damn thickheaded for your own good. Now you got the boss convinced that logic ain't gonna work."

I understood all too clearly. "So you take us to the cottage . . ."

Tolly giggled. "Hee hee. We take you to the cottage for a date. The cottage is far away from anybody, so you can make all the noise you want. Hee hee."

"Shut up, Tolly," Ray said. "We'll do him first." He gave Tolly his gun, the one he said had only one bullet in it. Tolly spun Monica around, got behind her, threw his arm across her throat, and held the muzzle of the forty-five close to her head. All routine. They had done this before.

"This is the way we do it," Ray explained. "You're way bigger than me, and you might be stupid enough to jump me. This way, if you make a move, poor old Mrs. G. is gonna have to scrape the chick's brains off the wallpaper." I let him handcuff me behind my back.

When Tolly saw I had been secured, he tightened his grip on Monica's throat, and pressed his body firmly against hers. Monica was taking big, ragged breaths. Her eyes showed white all around.

Tolly said, "Geez, Ray, she got a nice back." He dropped his arm from her throat so that his huge hand covered her breast. He traced its curve lightly with a calloused index finger. "Hee hee. She don't believe in bras. Hee hee. Guess she figures she don't need it."

He closed his hand tightly. Monica's face distorted with the pain. Tears squeezed from her eyes.

I clenched my teeth. Goldfarb hadn't sanctioned this kind of thing, I was sure, at least not yet, but there was a lot of accuracy in the comparison of Tolly with a Saint Bernard. With his master not around, he might go out of control. I didn't figure Ray to be much better.

"Moonlight on the beach," Tolly said, easing his grip. "I wouldn't mind that myself. How about you, Ray?"

"We'll see what the boss says," he said, putting the cuffs on Monica. I no longer considered him charming.

Monica's face was red, and she was standing rigid, eyes closed, trying not to scream or cry.

"She'd probably enjoy it," Tolly said. "What do you think, Cobby?" I wished Spot had bitten his testicles off.

"I have to go to the bathroom," I said.

"No stalling," Ray said.

"Look," I snapped, "I had a big meal. I personally don't care, but it's either here or inside the Imperial. Take your pick."

Ray saw my point. The car had the kind of plush upholstery an indiscretion would wreak havoc on.

"Okay. Take him, Tolly." He took his gun back from the giant.

"Upstairs," Tolly said.

"Wait a minute. How am I supposed to accomplish anything with my hands cuffed behind my back? Unless you plan to do it, Tolly? You seem to like touching helpless people."

He gave me a backhand across the face that Rod Laver would have been proud of. I spit blood on his shirt.

He was all set to give me another one, when Ray said, "Save it for later."

"I don't care if you shit in your pants," Tolly said.

The bathroom was at the top of the stairs, first door on the left. Tolly opened the door and motioned me inside with his gun.

"Aren't you going to come in and watch?" I asked.

"I ain't gonna let you get me mad. No reason to get mad at a dead man. Knock on the door when you're finished." He didn't tell me what with. "And don't be so long about it."

He shut the door behind me. I surveyed the place. The

132

window would have been too small to climb out, even if it hadn't had an exhaust fan in it. I wouldn't have left Monica, anyway.

I nudged the medicine cabinet open with the side of my face, and found just what I was looking for. "Basin Tub & Tile Cleaner," the can read. "Foaming Action." Beautiful.

The first thing I had to do was get my hands in front of me. I put my left knee on the edge of the bathtub, and squatted with my full weight on it, arching my back at the same time. After what seemed like days of strain and pain, my knee went pop! and I managed to get the cuffs hooked over the toe of my shoe. I inched my wrists forward a bit, then stood up.

My wrists were now linked below my crotch, my arms looped through my legs. Agonizingly, I contorted my body, cursing the long legs that had helped me in basketball but were a hindrance now. Finally, I could step through, and have my hands where they could be of some use.

I stretched for a few seconds to get rid of the kinks and cramps.

"Hey, what's keeping you?" Tolly's voice came through the door and scared me to death.

"I'm taking a dump," I said irritably. "Keep your shirt on."

I took the cap off the spray can of tub cleaner and put it down quietly on the sink. I cupped the can in two hands, and got my right index finger on the button. I was ready. Now it all depended on Tolly's reflexes.

"Okay, Godzilla," I called. "You can let me out, now."

"About time," he grumbled.

The door swung open. His face appeared at just about the height I'd figured it would. I pressed the button. He squeaked like a mouse as he caught a load of high-powered white foam dead in his eyes. The foam hissed and sizzled as it expanded.

Tolly's reflexes were in fine shape. He brought his hands up to his eyes in the normal human reflex. I dropped the can and squatted; then drove upward, smashing my two clenched hands and the steel cuffs with all the power my legs could generate into his groin. He produced a strangled scream that must have reached every dog on the East Side.

Tolly reacted with another normal human reflex. He

dropped his hands from his eyes and clutched at his genitals. He also dropped the gun.

I stood up and swung my iron-reinforced fists hard to his head, just under his right ear. He keeled over and pitched down the stairs, making a noise like a bowling alley on League Night.

From downstairs, I heard Ray yell, "What the fuck!" and the door of the study being opened. I picked up Tolly's automatic, and made a spinning dive that left me prone at the top of the stairs.

Ray saw me, and sent a slug from his big gun that hit the banister and showered me with splinters.

I pulled the trigger on Tolly's gun. Nothing. The safety was on. I didn't want to find out if Ray had been pulling my leg about having only one bullet. All ten of my fingers scrabbled along the sides of the little gun until the safety was found and clicked off. I jerked the trigger.

Ray grabbed his thigh and went down. I vaulted the railing, landed on my butt, stood up, and stomped on Ray's wrist as he tried to raise his gun. I kicked it away, and went to hit him.

Monica came out of the study and pulled me off him.

"Stop it. Matt, stop it. *Stop!*"

I stopped. I felt very weak.

"Are you all right?" I asked Monica.

She looked surprised. "Me?"

"Did he hurt you?"

"Oh, no, just a bruise."

Ray was rubbing his face against the carpet and making little crying noises.

Monica gulped. "You killed the other one," she said.

I stepped around to the foot of the stairs, where Tolly was lying very still. He certainly *looked* dead. I didn't want to touch him, but I had to find the key to the handcuffs, and I wanted to touch Ray even less; if Tolly was dead, I couldn't cause him any more harm.

The key was in his right front pocket. I unlocked the cuffs on Monica and me and threw them away down the hall.

"What happened while I was up there?"

"Oh, Matt, I was so scared, I—"

"Cut it out. We've got to get out of here as soon as we can. Ray didn't call anybody? Anything like that?"

"No, all he did was take a briefcase out of the wall safe. He said he didn't want to forget it."

"I want a look at it." I went into the study.

The briefcase looked as though it might be a real find. It was just a scuffed grey-leather case on the outside, but inside, it held a bunch of cloth-covered business ledgers. I flipped through one, but I couldn't understand the code Goldfarb used. I wondered why he had the books in his house, until I figured he was probably auditing himself. He was a top accountant, after all. I thought it was funny that he'd kept his real books in code, but stuck with the traditional red and black ink.

I put everything back the way I'd found it. "Okay," I told Monica, "let's go."

"There's no place like home . . . there's no place like home . . . there's no place like home . . ."

—Judy Garland, The Wizard of Oz
(MGM; seen on various networks)

17

There was a phone booth about a block away from Goldfarb's house. I checked my pockets, and found I'd used most of my change since I'd last been at my apartment.

"Got a dime?" I asked Monica.

"No. All my change was in my purse. I don't know where it is. I must have dropped it at the hospital."

"Damn," I said, "I have to use a quarter." I dropped the coin in the slot and dialed Homicide South. I had them connect me with Lieutenant Martin.

"Mr. M.?" I said when he picked up the phone.

"Matty? Where the hell have you been? We got some more questions for you. That Teobaldi woman hasn't been around, either."

"Never mind that. How anxious are you people to put Herschel Goldfarb away?"

The lieutenant sputtered. "What are you talking about?"

"Herschel Goldfarb, Accountant of Crime. Go to his house. There's a briefcase inside the study with a bunch of ledgers inside. I think they're his books, his *real* books. It can probably put him in Sing Sing. Or Danbury, if the Feds get their hands on it first."

"You forget I'm Homicide, Matty," he said slyly. "Why should *I* be interested in Herschel Goldfarb?"

"Ha," I said. "Ha, ha. Who is jerking whom, Lieutenant?" I asked him formally. "You know as well as I do Carlson was tied in with Goldfarb. And you also work with Detective Horace A. Rivetz, and know about his hangup."

"Yeah, I know it, but how do *you* know it?"

I was getting exasperated. "What the hell difference does it make? I'm handing you the bastard on a silver platter! If he gets back with his mother before you get there,

136

he'll burn that stuff. Right now, you don't even need a warrant, the door is standing wide open."

He thought it over for a second. "This wouldn't be a funny joke, you know, Matty."

"It's no joke, I promise."

"Okay, wait there, I'll get a couple of men there in a few minutes."

"I'm not there," I said.

A cab went by. Monica flagged him down, told him to start the meter and wait.

"Well, where are you, then?"

"I'll be at my apartment in an hour." I swallowed, and brought back a mental image of Tolly lying still on the stairs. "Lieutenant," I said, "Better bring an ambulance with you. There are two men hurt in there, one of them is pretty bad."

"Matty—" Lieutenant Martin began.

"Gotta go. Tell Rivetz *mazel tov*, he got Goldfarb," I said, and hung up.

I expected city employees to visit the apartment a lot sooner than an hour, so I told the driver to step on it. I wanted a chance to hustle Devlin out of there.

A lot of New York cabs have bullet-proof plastic between the front and back seats, as this one did. The driver was trying to say something, but he forgot to open the gizmo that made him audible to the passengers. Finally he remembered.

"Mister, there's blood coming from your mouth."

So there was, from when Tolly had belted me. I had gotten used to the taste. I wiped it on my sleeve.

Beside me, Monica started to tremble. I put my arm around her and let her get hysterical on my shoulder. She did it very quietly.

I was making soothing noises when I looked down and saw something that made me start to laugh.

Monica broke off her crying and asked indignantly what was so funny. She was an actress, after all, and I had broken into her big scene.

"We forgot your shoes," I said, pointing to her feet and ruined hose. Then we both laughed. It brought us back to normal.

When we were more sober, Monica said, "How does it feel, Matt?"

"My face? It's sore, what do you think?"

"No, not that. I mean . . ." She looked away.

"Killing a man, you mean?"

She flushed and turned back to me. "I'm sorry, Matt. I shouldn't have asked."

I squeezed her shoulder. "Forget it, it was a natural question. I shouldn't have snapped at you." I thought it over. "Basically, it feels rotten. I tried to talk us out of there. I almost waited until it was too late."

I felt her shudder. "I'm not sorry about it, Matt, just . . . stunned."

"I did it out of fear," I said.

"You didn't seem afraid."

"You just didn't notice. It's a preconception. Size-ism. No one over five eleven is supposed to show fear. Or feel pain. Or to be hurt by an insult, for that matter. It's as though people think body tissue is emotional armor."

"I never thought of that before," she said. "It just makes you that much braver." She kissed me on the cheek.

We were there. I saw no police around the building, but there was no telling how soon they'd be there. I paid the fare, and hurried Monica inside. I wanted Devlin out of that apartment. I had enough to explain already.

I shouldn't have worried. Devlin was gone. Without a trace. I checked the bedrooms to see if he was taking a nap. I checked the bathroom. I even checked the closets, to see if he was hiding, or even dead (which would have been a jolly thing for the police to find). He left no note. It was as though he'd never been there. Even the glass he drank Scotch out of had been washed and put away.

I ad-libbed a tirade for a minute or so, working in every cuss word in the book. Two or three times. How was I going to find him again?

"Well, at least he's tidy," I said, when my anger ran out of steam.

The apartment had "his" and "hers" bathrooms. I showed Monica hers, then went to his to wash the blood from my mouth and freshen up generally, then to my room to change.

Monica had freshened up, too, and was waiting for me in the living room. "Wait a second," I said when I saw her. I went to the master bedroom, which I seldom entered, where Rick and Jane had left all the stuff they couldn't take to Thailand. I went through Jane's closet and picked

138

out a pair of pumps in a soft brown leather, and brought them to Monica.

I knelt in front of her, took her foot to put one on. "Emily Post says one never entertains police lieutenants barefoot," I said.

"How do you know they'll fit?" she said.

"They're a half size too big," I told her, "but they'll do until you can get back to your apartment."

She was skeptical. "You remember my *shoe* size?"

"I remember everything," I said. I tickled the bottom of her foot to prove it. She giggled, and kicked the foot out of my grasp. Just as I got it back under control, and was about to slip the shoe on, the door swung open to reveal Lieutenant Martin and two uniformed cops.

"Well, well, how romantic. You're Prince Charming and she's Cinderella, right, Matty?"

Hoping I wasn't blushing, I took my time getting Monica shod, saying, "You didn't lock the door, did you, dear?"

"No," Monica said, playing along. "I forgot."

"That's all right. Spot's the one who insists on the doorbell, and he's spending the night with friends."

I turned to the police. "Okay, Mr. M., haul me in if you must. I'll call my lawyer from headquarters."

"Not so fast, sonny. We're going to have a talk. Man to man." He hooked a thumb at the uniforms. "Out in the hall," he said.

"But Lieutenant," they protested.

"Out! If he tries anything, I'll shoot him. Now, beat it!"

When the underlings had left, he said, "Mrs. Carls—excuse me, Miss Teobaldi, I mean. Matty and I are old friends. I'm the oldest friend he's got. You can go into another room, if you want, or you can stay, but Matty and I are going to have a talk off the record—my word on that—and Matty's gonna tell me exactly what went on at Goldfarb's tonight."

"I'll make coffee," Monica said. "Three sugars, right, Matt?"

"Right," I said. "I see you remember, too. Lieutenant?"

"Black, of course." He grinned.

I could see he was kind of uncomfortable. He was probably seeing me as a kid in jeans and a polo shirt, and finding it hard to get started.

I pulled him out. "Have you got Goldfarb?"

"Yeah, we were waiting for him. Why didn't you tell me he had his mother with him?"

"I thought I did. What's the difference, anyhow?"

"Because when his mother walked in and was greeted by two guys lying on the floor, an ambulance crew, and eight guys with guns drawn, she had an attack, collapsed, and had to be taken to the hospital along with the other two guys."

"Oh, Jesus, I never figured—is she all right?"

"Yeah, she'll be fine. They took her to Bellevue, she's sedated. They're keeping an eye on her."

I had a happy thought. "Hold it. You said with the other *two* guys? The big blond guy is alive?"

"He's alive all right, but he probably wishes he wasn't. You broke his neck, Matty. It's touch and go if you crippled him."

I felt sick. Tolly was a vicious creep, a human cockroach if you want; but even with a real cockroach, a person stomps on it, he doesn't pull its legs off.

"What about Ray?" I asked.

"The little guy? Close shave, there. Gunshot wound in the leg that came within a pencil line of some big artery, the doctor tells me. Lucky for everybody. Also broken wrist, broken nose, broken ribs. Nothing disastrous."

"Can he talk?"

"Oh, he's got a story all right, but I don't believe I buy it, Matty. I'm waiting to hear your story."

"What do you mean?"

"Look. These two guys, Ray Cali and Clarence Tolliver, have yellow sheets you can paper the wall with. There's a lot of leeway in the situation. The DA's office is ready to call it anything from Assault with Intent to Kill to Malicious Mischief, depending on what I tell him. And that depends on what you tell me."

Monica came back with the coffee. I looked the question at her.

"Whatever you say, Matt," she said.

I took a sip of the coffee while I considered it. The warmth felt good on the cuts in my mouth.

I put the cup down. "Okay," I said. "I have your word this is as far as it goes, and I've never met anyone whose word was better."

Lieutenant Martin made a point of putting his notebook in his pocket as I began.

"Goldfarb got on to me Tuesday night, my name leaked somehow."

"You can never plug all the leaks," the lieutenant said. "Somebody tells somebody who tells somebody, you know how it is."

I told him I understood. "Anyway, he slapped a tail on me as soon as I left Headquarters, but I shook it, and kept moving around so he couldn't pick me up again. I thought it was one of your guys.

"Goldfarb had decided I killed Carlson to have a clear field to Monica. He thought it over for a day or so, then grabbed Monica to force me to come over there."

It was all true up to there, and the lieutenant was buying it. He made grunts of assent at intervals through the story.

"Goldfarb held us there for a while," I went on, "but when he decided to take us far away from the city, I figured I had to do something."

"Okay, you did something. But even if you *did* kill Carlson, what did Goldfarb care?"

I shrugged. "Something about it being bad for business when a guy pays off and still gets killed. The other customers might take it amiss, might decide they'd be better off running than paying."

Lieutenant Martin shot a quick glance at Monica, but she was controlling her face.

"What does Goldfarb say?" she asked.

"Nothing. He won't let a word go between now and the end of his trial, except to his lawyers, you can bet."

"So what happens now?" I said.

"That's up to you. If you want to make a complaint for kidnaping, go right ahead, but it will mostly be your word against theirs. The way Ray tells it, you left before the trouble started."

The lieutenant patted his chest, then his sides before pulling a sorry-looking pack of Camels from his right jacket pocket. He looked around for an ashtray.

"Sorry, Mr. M., not an ashtray in the place," I told him.

"Yeah," he said, putting the pack away. "I forgot. Probably just as well I don't smoke it, I might live a few minutes longer."

"Just for laughs, why don't you tell us Ray's story," I reminded him.

"Laughs is right. According to him, he and Tolliver were just sitting around when five Puerto Ricans came in and tried to heist the suitcase. He said 'heist.' He started to say five niggers, but he saw me first. Anyway, they creamed Tolly with soap, but he managed to fight them off."

"Cute," I said.

"Very cute. Well, thanks for Goldfarb. I let Rivetz get his name on the arrest report, Goldfarb's been a damn Moby Dick to the guy."

"No charges against me?"

"Hell, you weren't even there at the time, right?" He paused at the door. "Oh, I almost forgot. Miss Teobaldi, one of the men found your shoes in Goldfarb's car. I'll have them brought to your apartment tomorrow." She thanked him.

When the door closed, I told Monica, "Call your credit card companies tomorrow."

She had borrowed a brush from Jane's room, and was sitting on the couch with her legs folded under her, brushing her hair. There's something erotic in the way a woman does that, a different tilt of the head, a different delicate arch to the body with every stroke. I wondered whether they do it the same way when no man is watching.

"Why should I call them?" she said, in response to my suggestion.

"You lost your purse," I said. "A junkie has it by now."

She stopped the brush in midair. "That's right," she said. She started stroking again, and paused again. "I have to call my producer, too, I missed a taping. Two of them." Again the start-stop. "Matt, will you come with me to see Tony in the hospital tomorrow?"

"Sure," I said. "I owe him that much. But don't you have to be at the studio tomorrow?"

"No, thank God, that little idiot I play isn't in the script for Friday. And frankly, I wouldn't care if she were."

"Careful," I said, "that kind of talk could cost you the part in 'Deadline.' "

"How do you know about that?" she demanded.

"Tony told me. Why shouldn't I know about that?"

"Well . . . I wanted to be the one to tell you. It's such a great opportunity, I mean if I get it, that I—"

"You weren't afraid I was going to talk you out of it again?"

She looked at the floor. "I think I was afraid I *wanted* you to talk me out of it," she said quietly.

"People do what they have to do, Monica. Or what they

want to think they have to do, if you follow me. The difference comes in how you go about it."

"I don't understand that at all," she said. Her face was very grave.

"Neither do I," I said, just as grave.

She laughed. "I don't care, it sounds profound. You should write dialogue for soaps."

"I'll use a pen name. How do you like Joy Fahwisk?"

"Not bad. How about a Chinese name—Tang Tide Fling?" We laughed.

After a while, Monica said, "Matt, I've got something I have to do. Or want to think I have to do."

"What's that?" I said, though I knew what she meant.

She didn't answer in words. She unfolded her long legs and kicked away the borrowed shoes. She stood barefoot on the carpet, and busied her hands on the buttons of the silk blouse.

I went to her and put my arms around her and kissed her. I didn't push her away this time.

"You in a heap o' trouble, boy."
—Joe Higgins, Dodge commercial

18

Well, I thought, at least my arm is asleep.

Monica's head was nestled in the crook of my arm, and the pressure of it had cut off the flow of blood to my right forearm and hand, giving it that ginger ale feeling that comes with obstructed circulation.

I looked at her sleeping face. Beautiful. For a sight like that, I could stand to let my arm get a little numb. The sheet had slid down to reveal half her smooth body. The bruise on her breast looked like an outward symptom of a broken heart. I had been very careful with it.

It had been *good*. It had been even better than before, slower, sweeter, less . . . desperate, I guess is the word. I should have been exhausted.

But I couldn't sleep. The tar pit was churning again, showing pieces of Vern Devlin on the surface, then sucking them down again.

It made me mad. I didn't like Devlin, and I didn't want him in my bed, especially now. It wasn't anything like fully formed thoughts, just a whiff of an idea that the right word would show me something important.

What did I know about Devlin? I didn't like him. He was a Scotch drinker. He had good eyes, recognizing me across Penn Station like that. I had told him to stay put, and he had taken off. He had been several hundred miles away from Carlson's murder. He gave me a pain in my ass.

None of that speculation contained the right word. I didn't know enough about him.

Then a soft black bubble broke the surface, whispering "maybe *Monica* knows the right word."

Maybe she did, at that, I thought resignedly. Hating myself thoroughly, I decided I had to ask her.

144

I thought I'd better try the light touch. I flexed a bicep rapidly, bouncing her head up and down.

"Mmmmm," she said. She smiled, but her eyes remained closed.

"Monica?"

"Mmmmm?"

"Monica," I said, "I want—"

"I know what you want," she said dreamily, then sprang into action. She sealed off the rest of the sentence with her lips, and proceeded to engage my attention so thoroughly that Vern Devlin was exorcised completely from my thoughts, thereby delaying the solution of the case for twenty-four hours. But it was worth it.

The face I shaved in the mirror next morning wore a sophomoric grin. I told it to stop, but it laughed at me. I finished shaving, dressed, went to the kitchen to work on breakfast.

I cut two lean slabs of ham, spread them with a mixture of lemon juice and apricot preserves, topped with maraschino cherries, and popped the whole thing under the broiler. I mixed up a couple of eggs with milk, sugar, nutmeg, and vanilla (my idea), then dipped slices of whole wheat bread (also my idea) into it to make my world-famous French toast. I had made this breakfast for Monica before.

I was flipping them over when Monica walked into the kitchen. She was sleepy-eyed and yawning and gorgeous in my terry robe that wrapped around her almost twice.

She laced her fingers above her mussed hair, stretched, and yawned wide enough to admit a grapefruit.

"You'll have to excuse me," she said, "I lose all my couth in the morning."

"All your couth, huh? You should meet Falzet. You'd think people in the communications industry would use the language better."

"Oh, shut up," she said rubbing her eyes. "What's for breakfast? Smells good." When I told her, she said, "I hate you. All this sweet stuff. I'll bet you never gain a pound. You shouldn't have a single tooth left, do you know that, Matt?"

I shrugged.

"I'll set the table," Monica volunteered. I directed her to plates and things, and she arranged them in the breakfast nook.

When she was getting the silverware, she said, "Don't you have a complete set of steak knives?"

"My French toast isn't all that tough," I assured her. "And you can cut this ham with a sharp look."

"It's not that," she said. "It looks like one's missing. See?"

She held up the rosewood case with the RSJ monogram on the lid, opening it to show the blue-velvet interior with niches for twelve ridiculously expensive steak knives. Only eleven of them were there, though. I had seen them all a couple of days before.

The ham was done. I got the mitten and took it out of the broiler. "It'll turn up," I told Monica. "I've been misplacing things a lot. I think it's creeping senility."

She laughed. "If last night was a sample of senility, I'm sorry I didn't know you when you were young."

"You couldn't have stood it," I informed her.

When we finished breakfast, we went to visit Tony at the hospital. His right leg was in traction, his left leg in a cast, resting on the bed. He went wild with joy when we walked into the room. He went wild wild with joy when *Monica* walked into the room. He didn't see me, and wouldn't have if I were a rhinoceros wearing a bow tie.

He said he was feeling fine, under the circumstances, and thanked me for getting him help so soon.

"Thank me?" I said. "Don't be foolish. You got me out of the way of that car, saved my life. Thank *you*."

He played the role like Gary Cooper. He did the whole humble hero bit short of saying "shucks, twarn't nothin'."

"I called in for you yesterday, Monica. Everything's straightened out at the show."

Monica kissed him on the forehead by way of thanks. They began to talk shop. I never felt so superfluous in all my life. I passed the time by trying to figure out why Tony looked so familiar today. Finally I got it. It was his eyes. He was looking at Monica exactly the same way Spot sometimes looks at me. That kid had it bad. I hoped I wasn't that obvious.

When it got to be lunchtime for the patients, a no-nonsense nurse came in and told Monica and me to leave. I smiled and nodded, the way I had done for the last half hour of the conversation.

Monica wanted to reciprocate for breakfast by making me lunch, but I told her I had to get back to work.

"Make sure you keep your doors locked," I warned her, "and don't pay attention to phone calls, all right?"

She said, "Don't worry, I've learned my lesson. Will I see you tonight?"

"I hope so." We kissed good-bye.

Heading back downtown, I tried to step back and see if I knew what I was doing, getting involved with Monica again. The verdict was probably not, but I felt so good about it, I didn't care.

The Network had gotten along without me while I was gone. The corridors were just as crowded, and the scenery was just as good.

Jasmyn Santiago was touching up her nails as I walked into Special Projects; she was using a silver-toned polish today.

"How many times a day do you *do* that, Jazz?" I asked.

"Oh, hello, Mr. Cobb," she said.

"Matt," I reminded her.

"Matt," she said. "Matt, Harris was in, he left you a note."

I took it from her and read it. The note said the green Ford with New York State License 297-VVJ was registered to an outfit called Big Apple Rent-a-Car, and that according to the company, the last they knew, it was at their lot at Kennedy Airport. Brophy was amazing. I wouldn't know how to go *about* finding out where one particular rental car was at any given moment. I had a hunch that however he did it, though, a secretary had been involved.

"Thanks, Jazz," I said. I was encouraged, because for once, I thought, she had given me the important news first. "Anything else?"

"Yes," she said, "some policemen are searching your office."

I said something along the lines of "Arrgh!" and asked, "They have warrants?"

"Of course. I wouldn't have let them in, otherwise."

I dashed into the office. The first thing to claim my attention was Spot, who went into the usual ecstasy routine the second he laid eyes on me. I said hello to him, then addressed myself to Rivetz, who I assumed was in charge of the search.

"What the hell is going on here?" I demanded.

He grinned at me. "Tried to throw me a bone, hey, Cobb?"

"What?"

"I appreciate the fact we got Goldfarb, I really do," he said, "but you got to be crazy if you think you can square a murder that way."

"Will you get to the point, Rivetz? What's going on here?"

He sighed. "Okay, might as well get down to business. Is your name Matthew Cobb, and do you reside at the following address?"

He read me my address. I told him I was and I did.

"Matthew Cobb, you are under arrest on the charge of Suspicion of Murder in the Second Degree. You have the right to remain silent. Anything you say, can and will . . ." he went on talking, but I tuned him out. They were actually arresting me. You have no idea what that feels like until it happens to you. It feels like Birdseye has flash-frozen your guts, and Johns Manville has stuffed your head with fiberglas insulation.

"Why?" I asked Rivetz. "Why now? What made the DA—"

He shook his head. "It was the lieutenant told me to pick you up. Didn't have the heart to do it himself." He shook his head again. "You really let him down."

"But why? What made him finally decide I killed Carlson?"

"Carlson? Cobb, I just arrested you for the murder of Mr. Vernon Devlin."

> *"Your Honor, I'm prepared to prove my
> client is innocent of these charges!"*
> —Raymond Burr, "Perry Mason" (CBS)

19

Lieutenant Martin made a noise like spitting. "I could kill you," he said. "You played me for a sucker, boy." He wouldn't say my name. He'd been yelling at me for ten minutes, and he still hadn't called me anything but "boy."

I hadn't been booked yet. Lieutenant Martin wanted to see me first, alone, in his office, for a little tête-à-tête invective.

"I let myself see you as a little boy, still, dammit! Well, I'll never make captain now. But that's not important."

I was sitting, he was standing in front of me. He bent over, and yelled six inches from my face, "Dammit, what am I gonna tell your Daddy? What is your Mama gonna do?" He made that spitting noise again.

"Don't do that," I said.

"Do what? Don't talk to me, boy."

"Cut it out, Lieutenant," I told him. "You see me as a little boy even *now*. I don't want to hear a lecture. I didn't kill Devlin; I don't even know how he died. Evidently you think otherwise. Fine. Either question me and give me a chance to clear myself, or for Christ's sake get me booked and locked up so I can call my lawyer—and cut out the outrage scene."

He was speechless with fury. I had never seen him like that before. His face was a mahogany mask, an ugly one. He strode back to me.

He was going to hit me. I could read it in his eyes and in the way he held his body. I wouldn't hit *him*, I promised myself, no matter what.

I met his eyes. I wasn't going to move, I wasn't going to blink. He raised his right fist, held it poised while he stared at me, then slowly brought it down.

He went back behind his desk and sat down.

"I have some questions I want to ask you, Mr. Cobb," he said hoarsely. "Do you give up the right to remain silent?"

"I do. I also waive my right to have an attorney present. Ask away."

He cleared his throat and began. The story came out in the questioning. A motorist heading east on the New England Thruway had reported a body lying in a gully alongside the road up in the North Bronx, just before New York City yields to Westchester County. The body was a male, late thirties or early forties, with documents identifying it as Vernon Devlin, of Fairfax, Virginia. He had been killed by a knife in the neck.

"This knife," the lieutenant said, shoving a photograph toward me. It showed a stainless steel blade with a horn handle; a steak knife, with the monogram RSJ on the handle.

"Can you imagine what I felt like when I saw that?" Mr. M. was getting personal again, but I let it pass.

"Couldn't have been any worse than I feel," I said.

"I don't need an expert to identify that knife, you know," he said. "I can do it myself. I know it came from your apartment—I mean your friends' apartment—because I recognize it from that dinner you cooked for your parents and me and Mrs. Martin and Cornelius and his wife at Easter."

I nodded. Certain cats were going to be let out of certain bags.

"Devlin took it from my apartment yesterday," I said.

"He did what? You trying to tell me Devlin was in your apartment yesterday?"

"Yes, he said he had some aspect of the case he wanted to discuss. I met him at Penn Station in the morning, went to NetHQ for a couple of minutes, then to my apartment."

"Yeah, we knew you were with him at the Network."

"Did you expect me to deny it?"

It was a rhetorical question, and the lieutenant didn't try to answer it. Instead, he said, "Some aspects of the case to discuss with you?" He scratched his head. "Isn't that a lot like what Carlson said?"

"Yes, it is."

"What aspects?"

I braced myself. "I can't tell you."

150

The explosion I was expecting didn't come. "You can't tell me?"

"No," I said. "I reclaim my right to remain silent for this question."

"It doesn't look good, you know," he said. I said nothing. "Okay, have it your way. When did you leave Devlin?"

"Just before noon," I said. "What time was he killed?"

"Between four and five."

"This morning?"

"Yesterday afternoon."

"Then what am I doing here?" I exploded. "*You* know where I was that time yesterday."

"I knew you were going to say that," he said. "Where were you that time yesterday?"

"At Goldfarb's house!"

He leaned back, lacing his hands behind his head. "Well, let's take a look at that, shall we? *You* say you were at Goldfarb's house. *Goldfarb* isn't saying anything. Ray Cali says he brought you there, but you left about one o'clock in the afternoon. Tolliver is still out of commission, in no shape to talk. How do I know you didn't kill Carlson, then go *back* to Goldfarb's house to find those two men beat up? You don't have much of an alibi after all."

"Well, what about Monica?" I protested.

"We have this saying around here," he said. " 'If she'll lay for him, she'll lie for him.' She's not going to do you much good with a jury, especially when we found a picture of you in his wallet."

He gave me another photograph to look at. It was a picture of me, which Devlin had sealed in plastic. I recognized it as the photo of me that had run in the April 2, 1973 issue of *Broadcasting*, along with the announcement in "Fates and Fortunes" that I'd been promoted to Special Projects.

"What's wrong with his carrying a picture of me?"

"It shows you had more to do with him than you ever admitted. It shows you've been covering up and are still covering up."

"What was my motive?" I challenged.

"I don't know, but we can damn sure prove you had one —I mean that you had it in for Devlin. You tried to hang a murder rap on him."

The lieutenant took out his cigarettes, put one in his mouth, struck a match. "Incidentally," he said between

151

puffs, "Rivetz is pushing to clear the Carlson murder with this arrest, too."

I didn't make a comment. My brain was running the word cigarettes over and over. Cigarettes, cigarettes. It was trying to tell me something, but what?

"What?" I said.

"I said," Lieutenant Martin repeated, "do you have anything else to say?"

"No," I told him. "What can I say?"

Sadly, he picked up the phone. "Tell Rivetz he can come book his prisoner."

This is it, Cobb, I told myself. Once again I asked myself the two Great Questions.

Rivetz knocked and entered. "Come along, Cobb," he said.

For once, I came up with an answer for question two. *"Wait!"* I barked. "The old lady! Mrs. Goldfarb! Has she been questioned? Has she had a chance to fix a story up with anybody? *She's* my alibi. Give her a line-up with me in it. She was there, ask *her!"*

Rivetz gave a snort, and pulled at my arm. "Come *on,"* he said.

"Hold it, Rivetz," the lieutenant said.

"Lieutenant," Rivetz pleaded, "don't *listen* to this guy. He's been playing on your goddam emotions the whole time. We can talk to the old lady any old time. Let me get him booked—"

"Shut up, Rivetz," the lieutenant said.

"But sir!"

"Shut up. I can wreck my career a little worse. My full responsibility."

Rivetz shut up, but he hated me worse than ever. He threw my arm down as though I were a rag doll. He backed up a few steps, but didn't leave the office.

The lieutenant picked up the phone again. "Get me Bellevue," he said. He was connected (at last) with the head nurse on Mrs. Goldfarb's floor. He asked if she was awake.

"She is?" he said. "Good. Has she seen anyone? Good. Thank you, good-bye." He reached for his jacket and hat. "You come with me," he told me. "Rivetz, you wait here for that operator, what's her name?"

"Gayle Spencer."

"Right. You meet her as soon as she gets here from

D.C., and whip her right over to the morgue for positive ID on Devlin. Question her, but don't be impolite."

In the lieutenant's car, heading for Bellevue, I solved the murder of Vincent Carlson for the second time. This time, though, I wasn't about to go off half-cocked. I was in for something much worse than mockery if I was wrong.

The clouds Cynthia Schick had noticed from her husband's hospital room two days ago finally delivered the rain they'd been promising. I looked at the fine droplets hitting the windshield, then being mowed down by the wiper blades as I ran through my theory step by step.

I turned the events of the last few days over and over—gingerly, like a drunk trying to gift-wrap an expensive bottle.

"Who is Gayle Spencer, Lieutenant?" I asked.

"Devlin's fiancée. He doesn't have any family living, so she gets the body."

"You said she was an operator?" I prayed for the right answer to this one. Operator, you see, had been the right word, the one my mind was groping for before Monica became so delightfully distracting.

"Yeah," the lieutenant said, "she runs the switchboard at CRI."

I turned my eyes to heaven. "Thank you, God," I said. "What?"

"Oh, nothing. One more question, if you don't mind. What happened to Devlin's glasses?"

"What are you talking about?"

"Devlin's eyeglasses. Did you find them?"

"No, because he didn't wear glasses. His license said he had twenty-twenty vision."

Mrs. Goldfarb was sitting up in bed when the lieutenant and I walked into her private room. She was eating chicken soup.

Her face became animated when she saw me. "Oh, Matt," she breathed. "Have you heard from my Herschel? Is he all right?"

"He's fine," I told her, "but he's under arrest."

"I know, I know. It's a good thing you and Monica left when you did! Somebody came and beat up Tolly and Ray, and the police, the stupids, arrested my Herschel. I can't even talk to him on the phone, and his lawyer is in the Virgin Islands. The doctor tells me don't worry, but I *have* to worry, I'm his mother."

153

"I'm sure everything will be all right," I said lamely. "I just came by to see if you were all right. I wanted to thank you for the wonderful dinner the other night."

"What other night? It was only yesterday, last night!" She made a face. "This is lousy chicken soup. How do they expect me to get well with lousy soup?"

"What time last night did you have dinner, Mrs. Goldfarb?" the lieutenant asked.

"Five-thirty, six."

"What about before that? Was Mr. Cobb there before that?"

"Yes he was, whoever you are. I was cleaning the hallway the whole time, all afternoon Mr. Cobb was at my house. I swear it."

The old lady folded her arms and set her chin. She gave off waves of virtue, like a transmitting tower. It was impossible not to believe her. At least I hoped it was.

Lieutenant Martin said, "Well, I don't mind saying that's a relief. Thank you, ma'am." He tipped his hat to the lady on the bed.

"You're welcome, whoever you are," she said.

The lieutenant signaled me to leave with him.

"Good-bye, Mrs. Goldfarb. I hope everything works out all right."

"It will if they let my Herschel go."

Let my Herschel go, I thought, a whole new battle cry.

On the way out of the hospital, the lieutenant said, "I'm sorry, Matty."

"Well you should be," I said. "You should have known better." I didn't mean it. In the same circumstances, I would have hauled me in. But I wanted to shake loose from police supervision, and the best way was to play on Lieutenant Martin's guilt feelings. It was the kind of move I always hated myself in the morning for.

"Well, it did look kind of bad against you," he said. "In fact, it still does. But I believe you, and I believe the old lady—I think *anybody* would believe that old lady—and that means somebody is out to frame you, Matty."

"I know."

"Who? Why?"

"I don't know who. I think the reason is I'm handy. Or maybe because somebody thinks I know who killed Carlson."

"You thought you did, too."

154

"So I did," I said cagily. "Well, just goes to show you."
I grinned at him.

What followed was a conversation without words, until
the very end of it when the lieutenant stated, "You're up
to something."

"I could be," I admitted, "if I weren't here."

"You want me to let you go." It wasn't a question.

"The old lady says I'm innocent," I reminded him.

"You want me to let you go."

"Remember the Broadway extortion case," I told him.

"Son of a bitch!" he said. "You actually *do* want me to
let you go!"

"Could you be worse off with the department than you
are now?"

"You're damn right I could! I could be hit with an
accessory rap!"

"Then forget it," I said flatly.

"You could escape," he said slyly.

"I'm not *that* sure of myself."

"You're pretty sure?"

I nodded.

"All right, then," he said, "get the hell out of here before I come to my senses." He turned his back on me, and
I was gone.

"To boldly go where no man has gone before."

—William Shatner, "Star Trek" (NBC)

20

My secretary keeps a diary on her face. As I walked into the office, I could see she'd been yelled at.

"Matt," she said, "Mr. Falzet wants to see you immediately. He sounded crazy!"

"More so than usual?" I said. "No calls, Jazz. Send Harris and Shirley to my office, assuming they're here."

"They're here, but Mr. Falzet—"

"Mr. Falzet can go slide down a barbed wire fence," I told her. I've been told I'm a much more decisive person when I know what I'm trying to accomplish.

Spot didn't want anything to do with me; I had deserted him for too long. He didn't exactly growl as I sat down, and he suffered himself to be petted, but he lay on the office floor in a sulk instead of acting like his usual hyperkinetic self.

He let me know I was being punished by playing up to Shirley when she came in. Brophy was right behind her, and got the same treatment.

"Another death-defying escape, I see," he said.

"You don't know the half of it," I assured him. "But there's no time for that. I think I'm about to get fired—"

"That *is* one of the rumors," Brophy said. "There's another one says you've been arrested."

"Both true. Now, for all I know, Falzet has the guards outside calling him right now to tell him I'm here, so I've got to talk fast. Here's what I want you to do . . ."

It couldn't have been staged better in a movie. Just as I'd finished saying, ". . . and I want them by this evening. One of those people is a killer," the phone rang. It was probably my imagination, but it seemed a particularly vehement ring.

"Cobb!" a voice roared in my ear.

156

"Yes, Tom?" I said cordially.

He was too mad to notice the familiarity. "I want you up here immediately, if not sooner!"

"Okay, I'll be there sooner."

Falzet said "What?" but I hung up on him.

"Harris, Shirley," I said, "thanks. I'll be in touch this evening. We who are about to die, and all that."

They wished me luck. I went up the stairs to Falzet's office.

"You wanted to see me, sir?" I said.

"You're through, Cobb!"

I shrugged. "Okay," I said, and started to leave.

He went wild. *"Come back here!"*

"Okay," I shrugged again. "Makes no difference to me."

"It may make no difference to you, but it does to the Network!"

It was a pleasure to be getting the boot. Now I could say things I always wanted to say, like: "Diagram that sentence."

"What?"

"I *defy* you to show me a diagram of the linguistic monstrosity 'It may make no difference to you, but it does to the Network.' You are a disgrace to the communications industry. No *wonder* Edwin Newman ran screaming off into the night that time at the Emmy Awards."

He was sputtering. "I'm . . . I'm . . . me . . . I'm a disgrace! I'm a disgrace! Look at this! Look at this headline!"

He thrust a *New York Post* at me. I had made the front page. The headline "NET V.P. HELD IN SLAYING" got second billing only to "Latest Track Results," which was printed *above* the mast.

"I'm a disgrace!" he said again.

"It could be worse," I told him.

"What could be worse than that!" He slapped the headline with the back of a hand.

"Buy a copy tomorrow," I told him.

The idea now was to get moving while he was still having his fit. I dropped through the Tower to the garage, where I checked out a car. I hoped to have it back before word filtered down. If not, and Falzet put out a complaint of Grand Theft Auto, my position would be that I had a contract, and I wasn't fired until I got my severance pay.

I had made a brief detour to Special Projects, ostensibly

157

to clean out my desk, but in reality to make it up with Spot by promising him a ride in a car. He loves that.

I got him stowed in the Network dinosaur, and took off for Kennedy Airport. While Harris and Shirley checked on the affairs of certain individuals, I wanted to see just who had rented the car that ran Tony over Wednesday night.

I didn't think it was one of Goldfarb's boys. Guys in that line of business figure it's easier and less messy to steal a car and then ditch it than it is to rent one. But for the amateur, I could see where renting a car for a hit-and-run would have a certain appeal. The rental company would obligingly eliminate the evidence of the hit-and-run, and if nobody got the license (and most times no one does), you'd be home free. And with any luck, the next day, someone else will rent the car, and take it to Boise, or Dubuque.

"It's enough to make *me* want Dubuque," I told Spot.

He didn't pay attention. He was using the car as a gymnasium, vaulting the seat, and standing on his hind legs to look out the back window. Then he found a switch for the power window with his paw, then jumped back yelping when the window hummed and started down. A little experimentation, and he had the window open all the way. He stuck his grinning furry face out into the drizzle, the way all dogs seem to love to do, and rode that way the rest of the trip.

They call the Long Island Expressway the World's Longest Parking Lot. The name is excruciatingly apt, especially at rush hour. I didn't let it get to me, though. I hummed along with the radio as I inched eastward, occasionally pulling a hair from the back of my hand, and chewing the inside of my cheek, where my souvenir of Tolly was healing.

The first terminal you come to on the incredibly confusing drive around Kennedy Airport is the one that houses El Al, Air India, and a few others. I drove up to it, dashed inside, and found the Big Apple Rent-a-Car desk. I asked the girl where they kept their records, and got directions to their main office and lot in a remote corner of the airport.

Spot was snarling at an airport cop when I emerged. I smiled at him, got in the car, and drove out from underneath the ticket he'd been about to stick on the windshield.

I managed to find the Big Apple lot without driving out onto any runways. When I got there, I told the young man at the counter what I needed.

"I'm not able to do that, sir," he said with a smile. He had lovely teeth.

"Come on," I coaxed. "I've got the license number of the car. I *know* you keep a record of who had what car when. All I want to know is who had it Wednesday night."

"I'm sorry, sir, I still can't." Employees of Big-Apple Rent-a-Car wore red blazers with green slacks or skirt, according to gender. I was willing to bet this clown had a worm in him. I took a ten dollar bill out of my wallet, and started fondling it on the counter top. He looked at it longingly.

"I'm sorry," he said at last.

"Too bad." I put the money away.

That was more than he could stand. "Well, I *could* check with Ms. Appleby."

"Who?"

"The supervisor," he explained. "She got promoted because of her name," he added in a whisper.

"Don't be catty," I told him. "Okay, it's a deal. Get me face to face with Ms. Appleby, and the money is yours."

He lifted a portion of the counter, and went through a door marked "PRIVATE." Through the door I heard a shrill voice saying, "From the Network? TV? Send him in, by all means!"

The boy with the teeth reappeared, waved me into the office, and stuck out his hand for the money. I gave it to him, even though the evidence suggested Ms. Appleby had been waiting all her life for me to show up.

"Hello, Mr. Cobb, is it? Larry has told me what you want, and I'm afraid it's quite impossible." She was another schoolteacher gone wrong; at least she looked like one, of the stereotypical repressed-spinster variety. She wore rimless spectacles, her dark-blond hair was drawn back in a tight bun, and she held her lips so tight they were almost nonexistent. She clashed with her stylish uniform. I had no doubt she'd soon rise high enough in the company that she could stop wearing it. She had the glint of the fanatic in her eyes.

I was about to find out one of the things she was fanatical about.

"However," she went on, "when I found out you were a vice-president of a television network, I wanted to ask *you* something."

"Shoot," I said resignedly.

"What is the name of the hopeless idiot who was responsible for the cancellation of 'Star Trek'?"

I run into these people all the time. I think Gene Roddenberry put some diabolical ultrasonic vibration on the sound track that had an addictive effect on certain people's minds.

"Ms. Appleby," I said, "not only was that almost ten years ago, it was another network entirely."

"That's not the point. I would think you would want people of some *intelligence* to watch television, too. Yet whenever a good program is on the air, you kill it. I hardly ever watch television for that very reason. Why, the only decent show that's been on since 'Star Trek' has been 'Harbor Heights,' and that only lasted a month!"

It was my turn to correct her. "Eight weeks," I said. "Tell you what. If you tell me who had that car Wednesday, I will personally see to it that 'Star Trek' is back on the air next fall."

"Can you do that?" She didn't dare let herself hope.

"Of course! I'm the vice-president, right? That show will be back on the air if I have to personally whittle Leonard Nimoy's ears into shape."

"Well," she said, "I suppose it's worth a try."

She addressed herself to one of several large filing cabinets. Big Apple wasn't quite big enough yet to have it all computerized. "Let's see," she murmured, "297-VVJ. Here it is."

I reached for the card, she pulled it away. "*I* will read you the name you want to know, Mr. Cobb. There's no need for you to know everyone who has rented that particular car."

I apologized, and took out a pencil and pad to write down what she was going to say.

I didn't need to write it down. "The customer who rented that Green Ford LTD Wednesday afternoon was . . ." she paused like a presenter at the Emmy awards, "a man named Walter Schick."

For an instant, I became the snot-nosed street kid I had once been. "Gimme that!" I snarled and snatched it from her hand.

There it was, big as life. "Name: Walter Schick. Residence: Greenwich, Conn." I dropped the card on the floor.

She swooped down on it like an eagle. "This is inexcusable, Mr. Cobb," she hissed.

"What?" I snapped, then realized what I was doing. "Don't mind me," I said affably, "I'm schizophrenic."

"Oh."

"What do you have to do to rent a car around here?" I asked.

"Well, please don't take this personally, but in your condition, I don't think it would be wise for us to—"

"I don't want to rent one," I interrupted. "Just tell me what the requirements are."

"A valid license. You need to be over twenty-one. And you have to be able to pay, of course."

"You always do," I said. I thought this new development over for a second. I didn't like it at first, but when I thought it over for a few more seconds, I hated it.

"Ms. Appleby, what would you say if I were to tell you the man who rented this car has been kept alive with the aid of a respirator since January? That he's been in a coma since then?"

"That's impossible!" she said.

"It certainly is," I agreed. "So it must have been someone else using Schick's driver's license. Lucky Connecticut doesn't use pictures on the licenses. Lucky for the killer, I mean."

"Killer?"

"Ms. Appleby, tell you what you do. Find out the name of the employee that rented out this car, at which terminal, and call me at the number on this card, and I will get you a part in 'Star Trek.' "

With stars in her eyes, she said she would.

"Live long and prosper," I told her, and left.

"Just one more thing . . ."
—Peter Falk, "Colombo" (NBC)

21

The drizzle had turned into a healthy adult-sized storm, and the sun had gone down. Willowdale hospital loomed out of the darkness like the cover of a Gothic novel. I hadn't bothered to phone ahead. Every damn crime in the case had been accompanied by a phone call.

I parked the car as near the entrance as I could. Spot squirted out of the car before I could close the door on him, and followed me into the hospital.

"Behave," I warned him.

It wasn't the same old lady behind the desk as was there Wednesday, but it might as well have been. This one was reading *Conan the Barbarian*, by Robert E. Howard. I figured someone was leaving these books around to have some fun with the volunteers.

"I'm looking for Dr. Fred Barber," I told her when she asked if she could help me.

"No dogs are allowed in the hospital, sir," she said.

"That's not a dog."

"Well, what is it then?"

"A toy. This is the first Bionic Puppy. Is Dr. Barber here?"

"Yes, he is. Would you like me to call him?" When I nodded, she picked up a microphone, took another look at Spot and said, "What will they think of next?" then paged the intern.

He walked into the lobby. I shook his hand, reintroduced myself, and said, "I'm glad you were here, I wasn't sure what shift you were working."

That made him laugh. "Interns don't have shifts, they have marathons. Are you looking for Mrs. Schick? She's in with her husband right now, if you want to talk to her."

"No, don't bother her. I just want to ask you one question: What was it you were bringing Mrs. Schick when I got here Wednesday?"

"What?"

"When I got here Wednesday, you were just coming out of Mr. Schick's room. You told me you had just brought something to Mrs. Schick. What was it?"

"Oh, that was nothing. Personal effects. There was some kind of power failure here when Mr. Schick was brought in, and in the confusion, his personal items got put in a carton and locked in a safe. Wednesday, she remembered to ask for them, that's all."

"What were these things?"

"You know. Shoes, keys, wallet—"

"No clothes?"

"His clothes were covered with blood. They were thrown away months ago. Look, I've got to get back to work . . ."

"Sure," I said, "thanks."

I took the Bionic Puppy back out to the car, and drove to the house on the Sound. Mrs. Locker answered the doorbell.

"Hello," I said politely. "May I come in?"

"Hello, Mr. Cobb," she smiled. "Come on in. I'll tell Miss Roxanne you're here."

"She's home?" I asked, surprised.

"You're calling on her, aren't you?" Agatha asked, logically.

"Of course," I lied. "I'm just glad she's here."

Roxanne joined me downstairs in a couple of minutes. She was wearing a hooded sweatshirt and faded blue jeans. I wondered what she looked like in a dress.

"I'm flattered, Cobb," she said. "To come all this way on such a terrible night."

"I thought you weren't going to let your mother go alone to the hospital anymore," I said.

She looked exasperated. "I can't lock her up, you know. She happens to own this house. If you must know, I was going to go with her, but she skipped out while I was taking a shower. Okay?"

"All right," I said. I figured I had more important things to worry about. "Rox, I want to take a look around the house."

"Okay," she shrugged. "What are you looking for?"

163

"A hole," I said, "among other things. Do you happen to know where your father's wallet is?"

"It's at the hospital, isn't it?"

"No, your mother got it back Wednesday. I think I'll start upstairs. Care to tag along?"

"I think I will," she said. "I don't want you to steal anything."

I checked the master bedroom first. There was nothing in the clothing drawers except clothing. I opened Walter Schick's closet, and saw nothing but his suits hanging there, going quietly out of style. There was no wallet in that room. I gave up looking for it.

"The study next," I told Roxanne.

"Cobb, what are you up to?" she asked.

"You don't want to know, Twerp. Any sooner than you have to, anyway."

"It's about Dad, isn't it?"

"Yes," I said.

"He did something terrible, didn't he?"

"I'm afraid so."

"Why can't you leave him alone? Hasn't he been punished enough? What more can you do to him?"

"It's not only him," I said. "Look, Roxanne, the other day you gave me a little lecture. Now I'll give you one. You're going to have to be brave, maybe as brave as you were when you kicked dope and stayed off. But it's got to happen, or things will only be worse. Even if you hate me for it, its *still* got to happen."

"I won't hate you," she said.

The study had the musty smell of the closed-off wing of a museum. It seemed bigger without Walter Schick in it, than it had when he and I had had conferences here. I knew the room fairly well, and I made a beeline for what I wanted to see, the bound editions of *Broadcasting* magazine, the television industry's bible, that were kept on the bookshelves. It was said that Walter Schick had sped his rise to the top by memorizing important articles in *Broadcasting,* and having facts always ready.

I pulled the green-bound volume marked JAN–APR 1973 down from the shelf, and turned to the April 2 issue. The "Fates and Fortunes" section had a page missing, the page my picture had been on.

"Damn," I said.

"What's the matter?"

"I found the hole. I wish I could crawl into it." I slammed the volume shut, put it back on the shelf. "Rox," I said, "I'm going to finish this tonight, for better or worse, probably worse. Do you want to come along? It might be better to get it over with."

She swallowed, but when her voice came, it was smooth. "Yes, for God's sake, let's get it over with."

I sat at Walter Schick's desk and made some phone calls. The first went to the switchboard at NetHQ, merely to ascertain whether Mr. Hewlen and Mr. Falzet were working late tonight, as planned. They were.

The next call went to Manhattan Homicide South and Lieutenant Martin.

"I'm ready," I told him.

"Ready for what?" he wanted to know.

"To cover you and the department with glory. I'm ready to solve this goddam case, and incidentally, to throw my entire life down the toilet at the same time."

There was silence for seven seconds. Then, "Jesus, Matty, are you *confessing?*"

"No-oo! Look, the best way to do this is to get this Gayle Spencer—she did make it to town?"

"Yeah, she's here."

"Good, she's important—she's *vital* to the case. Get her, and meet me at the Network building in half an hour."

"Yes, Mr. TV Detective, sir. Anything else I can do for you? Do you want me to bring Goldfarb along?" His voice dripped sarcasm.

That was an interesting thought. The more I thought about it, the more interesting it was. "Yeah," I said finally. "Yeah, bring old Herschel along."

"If I do this," the lieutenant said, "I'm just as crazy as you are, you realize that."

"If we're crazy, they can't put us in jail," I said.

"That *is* a consolation," he said. "Okay, when do you want to meet, again?"

"Half hour, NetHQ. It'll work out," I assured him.

The next call went to the hospital to tell Mrs. Schick I had something important to tell Mr. Hewlen, and I wanted her to be present when I did so. I said I'd be by to pick her up.

Next, I tried to call Monica. If you're going to stage a William Powell–type denouement, you might as well make

165

sure all your characters are present. Unfortunately, Monica was neither at her place nor at my place. I didn't try Tony's room in that Manhattan hospital. I'd just have to struggle along without her.

"You are murderer!"
—J. Carroll Naish,
"The New Adventures of
Charlie Chan" (syndicated)

22

Only one exchange of any consequence took place on the ride back to the city. It happened just before we picked up Mrs. Schick.

Cobb: What happened to that money you inherited last summer?

Roxanne: My father bought me a bond.

Cobb: Are you sure?

Roxanne: Of course. I clipped a coupon just last month.

That was it. After Cynthia Schick got in the car, I don't think more than ten words were spoken, the last two being "We're here." I said that. Oh, and Spot barked when I locked him in the car.

Several police cars were parked illegally, and I cuddled the Network car close in behind them. They were early. I hustled the Schick women across the plaza. The plaza fountain spouted water into the sky in a pathetic effort to fight back the rain. I could sympathize with it.

In the lobby of the Tower of Babble, there was an informal gathering around the security desk. I recognized most of the people there. There was Wilkie the guard, Lieutenant Cornelius U. Martin, Jr., Detective Horace A. Rivetz, who was handcuffed to Herschel Goldfarb, a couple of subordinate plainclothesmen, and a few uniforms. The petite redhead in the green dress had to be Gayle Spencer, Devlin's fiancée.

"You're late," the lieutenant said.

"No, I'm not. Miss Spencer?" I said to the girl. "Matt Cobb. I'm glad to meet you." She didn't extend a hand, and I was just as glad, to tell the truth.

"I wish I knew what was going on," Miss Spencer said, with a frown that made her freckled face crease. "I have arrangements to make."

I didn't get a chance to answer her. "Mr. Cobb is going to reveal the murderer of your fiancé, Miss Spencer," Lieutenant Martin said. There was an interesting undertone in his voice, made up of equal portions of "please?" and "you damn well better!"

Cynthia Schick said, "Oh, really? Does my father know about this?"

Wilkie the guard, who had been with the Network for as long as I'd been alive, answered for me. "Yes, ma'am. I called him on the house phone when the officers first got here."

Now Goldfarb had a question. "What am I doing here? I demand to see my lawyer."

"Shaddap, Ozzie," Rivetz told him, just on general principles.

"Relax, Goldfarb," I said, finally getting a chance to answer a question addressed to me. "As far as I'm concerned, you're here as an interested spectator. I don't have a single question to ask you, I just thought you might appreciate a night on the town, instead of being cooped up. It's up to you."

He gave that hateful chuckle again. "In that case, I'll stay."

"Terrific. Lieutenant, I have to stop at my office for a second. I'd appreciate it if you would take everybody upstairs to Mr. Hewlen's office. I'll join you there in about five minutes."

"Why?" he demanded. "So you can make an *entrance*, for God's sake?"

I grinned at him. "What do you expect from a TV man?"

He just shook his head and walked away, muttering something about being in too deep. I wondered what he would have said if he'd known I was stopping at my office hoping to find evidence that would prevent my case from being blown away like the Flying Nun.

Harris and Shirley were waiting in the Special Projects office.

"What have you got?" I asked them.

"All of it," Brophy said. "I thought I was kidding the other night." He laughed.

"It's just like you said, Matt," Arnstein told me. "What do we do now?"

"How fond of your jobs are you? If I do all the talking up there, somebody's going to realize how much this case depends on my unsupported word. Care to play Saul and Fred for me?"

"What?" Shirley said.

"Never mind. Care to come up and supply the vital information at the vital moment?"

"Sure," Harris said. "I wouldn't miss this for the world. Besides, Jimmy Carter has promised to make us a job anyway."

I looked at Shirley. She nodded. "Great," I said. I glanced over the facts they had gathered, then led the parade upstairs.

There was a bunch of bewildered people in the anteroom of Mr. Hewlen's office. While I had remembered Mr. Hewlen telling Falzet they'd be screening pilots tonight, it had never occurred to me that the *program* staff of the Network would have to be there, too. You can't think of everything.

The three of us ran a gantlet of curious stares to the office door. I opened it and went in. The room was silent as we walked to the stagelike platform where Mr. Hewlen's desk was.

When I was close enough to him so he didn't have to shout, the Chairman of the Board said, "What is the meaning of this, Cobb?"

"You've lost your rocker, Cobb," Falzet said. "I told you you were fired."

"True," I admitted, "but I have a duty left to perform. I was ordered by Mr. Hewlen to find out who was responsible for messing up the CRI ratings, and causing 'Harbor Heights' to be cancelled."

I backed around toward the ceiling-to-floor windows, to have rain-swept Manhattan for a backdrop. My audience was in a ragged semicircle: Mr. Hewlen at his big desk on my extreme right, Falzet in a leather chair, Roxanne standing, Harris Brophy next to Roxanne, Goldfarb in a chair, Rivetz standing next to him, Lieutenant Martin standing alongside the chair occupied by Cynthia Schick, Gayle Spencer and Shirley Arnstein on a love seat that matched the chairs.

"Does everybody know everybody?" I asked. Lieutenant Martin did the honors. He might have felt he was sinking fast, but by God, he was going to sink with style.

"Get on with it, Cobb," Mr. Hewlen said.

"Yes, sir." I cleared my throat for effect. "Actually, the

169

big problem in solving this case was that there were so many crimes involved, it was hard to know which ones made any difference.

"Now I know that there were five interconnected crimes: fraud (the ratings gimmicking), blackmail, two murders, and an attempt on *my* life.

"It cleared away the deadwood. Now I am absolutely sure Walter Schick's accident *was* an accident. And I know why Devlin was killed."

Lieutenant Martin broke in. "Why *was* Devlin killed?"

"Because he knew who killed Carlson, and why."

"Well?"

"I'm coming to that," I said.

The lieutenant shrugged and looked heavenward. I ignored him.

"This whole dismal thing started," I began. "Well . . . it's hard to say when it started. It started either when Vincent Carlson became so desperate for money he had to rape the broadcasting industry for it, or when Walter Schick and his wife became tired of waiting to see who would succeed Mr. Hewlen as President of the N—"

"*You take that back!*" Cynthia Schick was livid.

"Cobb! How dare you—"

"Save it, sir," I said, not disrespectfully. "It gets worse.

"Anyway, when *both* of these things happened, a deal was made. If 'Harbor Heights' were to fail, Walter Schick would certainly be made President of the Network. That's the way it worked out, you'll remember.

"I'm not sure who approached whom . . ."

"Schick approached Carlson," Rivetz said. He drew everybody's eyes, and seemed surprised at himself. "I did some checking up at this Network," he said. "If it was Carlson who made the deal, it would be more natural for him to go to Falzet, who was in charge of programming. Of course, this is just figuring," he added sheepishly.

I smiled. I was delighted to find an ally in such an unexpected place. "True, but you probably don't know that Carlson (and Devlin for that matter) knew Walter Schick personally, from the time the ARGUS system was being installed at CRI. Which, by the way, Mrs. Schick lied to me about. She said she never heard of Carlson and Devlin, and she said she 'doubted' her husband knew them. Two different witnesses told me both Mr. and Mrs. Schick knew them both." I *didn't* say that one witness was Monica (who

170

in fact never said anything about Cynthia Schick at all) and the other one was Devlin. I did suggest to Lieutenant Martin that he ask Miss Spencer about the matter.

I didn't give him time to do it right then, though. The idea was to keep everybody dazzled with footwork until I was finished, and hope by that time Lieutenant Martin would have enough pieces to build a court case out of. Airtight evidence is *hard* to find.

"There is no doubt that the ratings *were* tampered with," I went on. "I'll tell you how." Devlin was good at explaining things, I have to give him that. I let them have the explanation he had given me Thursday morning, practically verbatim.

Lieutenant Martin whispered a word to one of the detectives, who nodded and left the room. "I sent a man to check," he said. "Matty, this is the wrong way to go about this. I want to talk to you, *in private.*"

Then came a moment I'll treasure for the rest of my life; Falzet shushed him, fascinated (he'd been the one shafted, after all), and wanting me to go back to the story. The lieutenant was so surprised, he *did* stop talking.

Before astonishment could change to rage, I stepped into the breach.

"Now we all know what happened in January. Walter Schick drove off that road and is now little more than a vegetable."

Roxanne was staring at me: she'd never seen Matt Cobb like this before. It was as though one of the plants in her living room had talked back. "I thought—" She gulped and started again. "I thought you said that was an accident."

"I did. But, Roxanne, what happened before your father left the house? What did you say must have happened?"

"Roxanne!" It was a command from her mother, a plea from her grandfather.

She glanced at each of them, then returned to me.

"You don't have to say, Rox," I told her. "Mrs. Locker can tell the police from her own knowledge."

"They had a fight!" Roxanne said. "Big deal! I said my Dad must have been upset to have an accident, that's all."

"That's all," I said. "But something else started in January. Shirley?"

"Huh?" she said. "Oh, right. On January fifteenth, Mrs. Schick withdrew ten thousand dollars from the State National Bank of Connecticut. On February fifteenth, she

171

withdrew ten thousand dollars from the Fairfield County Trust Company. On—"

"Sum it up, Shirley."

"Okay," she said, checking her notes. "Every month since January, Mrs. Schick has raised ten thousand dollars in some way. *I* haven't been able to find out what she did with it. Fifty thousand dollars, so far."

Cynthia Schick was gathering herself up, waiting for me to say the awful word, so I didn't. I let the room be quiet, and the cops, no fools they, did the same, waiting for someone to have a revelation.

It came to Mr. Hewlen. Quite wonderingly, he whispered, "Blackmail."

"A blackmail demand came on January eleventh, Mrs. Schick?" I asked gently.

She looked as though she wanted to deny it but couldn't find the strength. At last she nodded.

"Is that what Walter and you argued about? Before Roxanne called and he went out?"

Her face was dead. Looking at a point three feet above my head, she said, "Walter was furious, just furious. He said he was going to have it out with Father the next morning. He wasn't going to pay, he wouldn't stand for it, he—"

"Cynthia . . ." her father warned. "Lieutenant, I demand this farce be stopped! Cobb is making dangerous and illegal allegations!"

Mr. M. made the old man wait while he lit a Camel. "Actually, you may as well let him finish, Mr. Hewlen. If he's not right, he's committed enough slander to keep him in jail until Fire Island gets a pro football team."

"But he's accusing my daughter of *murdering* this Carlson because he was *blackmailing* her!"

"Excuse me, sir," I said. "That wasn't what I was getting at at all."

"No?" Rivetz said in surprise.

"Not at all. Carlson wasn't the blackmailer, and Mrs. Schick didn't kill him."

"Then who—" The lieutenant dropped his cigarette, it rolled to the feet of Goldfarb, who had been watching the whole performance with a beatific smile on his face. With his free hand, the ex-professor picked it up and handed it to the lieutenant, who did not thank him.

"Then who—" the lieutenant said again.

172

"Devlin," I said. "Harris?"

"Vernon Devlin opened accounts at six banks and savings and loan associations in the greater Washington, D.C., area, to the tune of about twenty-seven thousand bucks, since the beginning of the year. In addition, he moved to a new apartment, and his fiancée has been driving a new BMW to work." It figured Harris would have something extra like that to throw in.

"Thank you," I told him, then addressed the whole gathering. "If you want to know how Devlin found out, it's very simple. Devlin had an inkling, approached Carlson, and Carlson *told* him. Carlson was like that, ask anybody who knew him. Yes, Miss Spencer? Did I say something wrong?"

The CRI operator was sucking air in like a pubescent girl warming up for a hyperventilation fit. "You're not going to get away with this!"

"Yes, I am." It's always a good idea not to say what they expect you to say.

It shocked her out of her fit. "You admit it? You admit you're trying to pin it on Vern because he's dead?"

"Of course I'm trying to pin it on him. He did it."

"You can't prove it. Those bank accounts aren't proof."

I had to admit she was right. "No, I can't prove he black-mailed Mrs. Schick."

"Aha!"

"All I can prove is that with your help, he murdered Carlson."

Hell broke loose in the office. I was rather proud of myself. Cynthia Schick was horrified. Lieutenant Martin clapped a hand to his head. Roxanne looked puzzled. Falzet kept looking around himself, saying "ludicrous" to anyone who would listen. Goldfarb threw back his head and laughed. Rivetz grabbed him by the collar and shook him. It was his position that Goldfarb had no right to enjoy anything, at any time.

Gayle Spencer drew back as from an electric shock. Mr. Hewlen bellowed, "Martin, I'll have your badge if you don't get this madman out of here!"

But the lieutenant said, "Well, you blew it, Matty, it was fun while it lasted, but how can you explain that alibi of Devlin's? How did he fool you, Rivetz, *and* the phone company computer?"

"Come on," I said. "Didn't this whole mess come about

because Carlson diddled the CRI computer? This one was even easier to fake.

"Devlin bothered me from the first time I spoke to him, Lieutenant Martin and I have already discussed that. His apparent attitude didn't match his actions. He begged me to keep his name out of the problem, then kept the line open until he could speak to the police.

"I came up with a theory, a really beautiful one, that said Devlin had hired a woman to impersonate an operator, and had called from a booth near the Hotel Cameron. Of course, the phone company and their famous computer put that out of the question.

"Miss Spencer, did Devlin smoke cigarettes?"

The redhead looked surprised. "What has that got to do—oh, okay, yes, he did."

"That can be checked, of course, Lieutenant, but I believe it."

"Naturally," he said drily. "It suits your theory." It drew a few random chuckles from the gathering.

"Find any cigarettes on the body? I say there weren't any."

Rivetz told me I was right.

"Well, that's how I got back on to Devlin as the killer. I was with him for a short time Thursday, about an hour and a half, and during that time he must have gone like this"—I showed them the body-patting routine—"seven or eight times. He *said* he was looking for a pair of glasses, but I found out later that was a lie. According to the police, Devlin's license says he had twenty-twenty vision. He was looking for his pack of cigarettes. I realized that when I saw Lieutenant Martin pat his body the same way. Smoking is a filthy, stupid, disgusting habit, but it *is* a habit, it's not usually done consciously. Lieutenant Martin didn't remember what pocket he'd put his pack in. Devlin didn't remember he didn't have any cigarettes on him."

I beat everybody to the obvious comment. "Big deal, right?

"The big deal was that when I asked him about it, he *lied*. Why the hell should he lie? I am personally of the opinion that tobacco is the Red Man's Revenge, but Devlin couldn't know that. Even if he did, who was I to him? What did he care what I thought?

"The only explanation, or at least the only one my limited resources can come up with, is simply that Devlin didn't

174

want anyone to know he smoked, anyone connected with the case, I mean. Because the police lab had determined that two people had been smoking in Carlson's room at the hotel. Carlson was one, the murderer was probably the other.

"It could be that Devlin didn't want to leave a butt around for analysis. I know they can type blood from saliva samples. I don't know if they can make positive identifications, but I wouldn't bet my life they couldn't, and Devlin wouldn't either. I say he knew he was an unconscious smoker, so he made sure he didn't have anything on him to smoke.

"But the fact remains, if he was so concerned about smoking, he must have been the one who smoked the cigarettes with Carlson at the hotel."

"Very clever, Mr. Cobb," Herschel Goldfarb said. "Brilliant, in fact. But it all rests on your unsupported assertion that this body-patting took place at all."

"Shut up!" Rivetz barked.

"No, it's okay," I said. "Your point is well taken, Mr. Goldfarb, but I'm not presenting legal evidence. I'm describing the way events and my thoughts *led* to the evidence."

"I see. Sorry to have interrupted. Please continue." Goldfarb smiled graciously and leaned back in his chair.

"Actually," I went on, "a lot of this thinking was filled in later. The solution of this case came big end first, this afternoon, when Lieutenant Martin mentioned that Devlin's fiancée, Miss Spencer, was the switchboard operator at CRI. Then the answer was as obvious as a pimple on Telly Savalas's head. Want to tell them how it was done, Miss Spencer?"

"Don't say anything," the lieutenant warned her. He read her her rights. "Okay, Matty," he said when he finished. "I think even *I* could line it out from here. You don't need her."

Gayle Spencer was single-mindedly exercising her right to remain silent. Her freckled jaw was firm, but her eyes were jumping around.

"Okay," I said, "but I don't think she was in on the planning. I think Devlin killed Carlson because Carlson was having conscience trouble. He was going to tell what he did. He came to me, which was his tough luck.

"Knowing Carlson, I think it's reasonable to assume he

175

told his pal Devlin that he was going to blow the whistle on himself and, for Devlin's own protection to forget he had ever been in on the secret. Carlson was too nice a guy.

"Because he didn't know about Devlin's hundred-twenty-thousand-dollar-a-year hobby. Devlin *couldn't* let Carlson talk. Not only would the money be gone, but if Carlson talked, Mrs. Schick had nothing left to protect. You can bet Devlin would have gone down, too."

I had them, now. There's a feeling in the atmosphere when everyone's attention is on you and nothing else. They were all almost holding their breaths waiting for what I would say next. I was enough of a ham to enjoy it.

"When Carlson came to New York—because I was here—Devlin moved. He set up what I'm sure he told Miss Spencer was a practical joke, then followed Carlson.

"Tuesday night, Devlin sneaked into the Hotel Cameron, to Carlson's room, and tried to talk him out of telling the story, without success, so regretfully—I'm sure it was regretfully—he stabbed his friend in the back with a switchblade knife, and began wiping his fingerprints from the room.

"He was just finishing up when I walked in. He beaned me with an ashtray, wiped it again, and left to put his alibi into operation.

"Now the idea was to get it established with the police that he was in Washington, D.C., a couple of hundred miles away, at the time of the murder. Of course he wasn't, *but his voice was.*"

Rivetz broke in. "Are you trying to say it was a recording? It wasn't, you know, it answered questions, for God's sake."

"No, it wasn't a recording. In fact, maybe I was wrong to say his voice. What we heard was electromagnetic waves generated by his voice recondensed and reamplified to sound like his voice."

Rivetz still looked bewildered. Lieutenant Martin said, "Look, it's simple. Devlin conks Cobb, then goes outside to a phone booth. First, he calls the precinct, with the anonymous tip about the body. Then he calls this chick at CRI—"

"Collect," I said. "On a WATS line."

"Yeah, so he wouldn't have to keep shoving coins in the phone," the lieutenant continued. "So the Spencer woman takes the call right there at the . . . what do you call it, with the holes?"

"Patch rack," I said. "Or switchboard, I guess for telephones. Doesn't matter, it would work with one of the new push-button systems like the one we have here at the Network, too. All she did was this: She took the output of Devlin's call from New York, and plugged it into another outside line. Then *she* dialed the number of the Hotel Cameron, and presto, the phone company computer says the call we got from Devlin came from D.C., as of course it did. It *didn't* tell us about the first leg of that call, coming in from New York at the same time, but only because we didn't ask. There's your evidence. That call will still be in the computer, and if he *did* call collect, there may be a living long-distance operator who can remember taking the call.

"Any comments, Miss Spencer?" I said.

"Yes," she said. "Vern said it was only a practical joke and . . . and I guess I want a lawyer."

Lieutenant Martin told one of the detectives to take Miss Spencer to Headquarters and see about getting her a lawyer.

"Of course," I concluded when they were gone, "as soon as he finally got the phone call through, Devlin hauled out to the airport and got a plane back to D.C. in time to be interviewed by the local police the next morning. What is it, an hour flight? Not a hundred and eighty-six thousand miles a second like the telephone, maybe, but plenty fast enough.

"It would have stood up, probably, but I was involved in the case. I'm not bragging, far from it, I was in the dark for a long time. But paranoia set in, for the killer *and* for me. The killer wanted to neutralize me, for fear of what I'd find out, and I had to keep digging for fear of what the killer would do to me.

"So that hit-and-run attempt was made. Lieutenant, you don't happen to know off the top of your head where Devlin was Wednesday night, do you?"

"No, why should we?" he said. "At the time, we figured he was clean."

"I can give you a pretty good idea of what he did. He flew to New York during the day and rented a car from the Big Apple outfit. Then, he staked out either my apartment or Monica Teobaldi's, more likely mine. He followed

177

me and a friend of mine for blocks, looking for a clear shot. When he got one, he blew it. He drove into Tony Groat instead.

"The only thing to do then was to drive the car back to the airport and fly home. The next day, he took the train up to New York. He couldn't have stayed overnight in New York, because he had to be home to talk to the police if they wanted him. I brought him to my apartment, and shortly after I left him, he was killed."

"That's what *you* say," the Chairman of the Board said. "It sounds—this whole *circus* sounds like an attempt to cover up the fact that you killed the two of them. Martin," he began ominously.

"Cut it out, Mr. Hewlen," I said. "This is serious. You know your daughter killed Devlin."

That surprised everybody but the cops. Roxanne Schick goggled. "You're kidding, right, Cobb? I mean, my . . . she . . . doesn't have murder in her."

Cynthia Schick might have been in church, from the look on her face. It was the serene look I'd seen twice before, at the hospital, and here in this office, last Wednesday.

I was talking to Roxanne, but looking at her mother. "Of course she has murder in her," I said. "Don't be foolish, Roxanne. She murdered 'Harbor Heights.' She tried to murder Tom Falzet's career. Along with your father, she's murdered the Network, maybe the whole industry. It will never recover from this. Just because of the ambition and greed of Walter and Cynthia Schick—"

"That's a lie!"

It happened. Cynthia Schick's composure had snapped. She leaped from her chair, and warily, as though backing away from a predator, edged toward the windows.

In a different way, she became as much a caricature of herself as her husband was. Where life had redrawn him as an infant, she took on the appearance of a rabbit; nostrils wide and twitching, eyes liquid and wide, body trembling, wary and fearful in every nerve.

"That's a lie!" she said again. *"Tell* him, Father. Tell all of them! I don't want them to say that about Walter, please, Father, make them stop, please."

"Cynthia, I—" he began helplessly, and more than a little fearful himself.

"I'll admit what I did. I *did* kill Devlin, I don't care who knows about that! He was dirt. But they can't think

178

those terrible things about Walter, tell them, Father, tell them how good Walter was for the Network."

Mr. Hewlen was suffering, and he wasn't used to it. It's not easy to watch your daughter go off the deep end in front of your eyes.

"What . . . what do you want me to say?"

Cynthia Schick's attention was concentrated on the old man. Lieutenant Martin edged closer to her. There was no telling what she'd do in that condition.

"I want you to tell them—*get away!*" She saw the lieutenant move, and jumped back, thudding against the brown glass windows. Like a frog's tongue, her hand was in and out of her purse.

There was a clicking noise, and a silvery arc in the lamplight.

By the time action slowed enough to be perceptible, I could see Lieutenant Martin holding a bleeding hand, and Cynthia Schick holding the point of a pearl-handled switchblade against her throat.

*"You are about to enter another dimension
. . . a dimension not only of sight and sound,
but of mind . . ."*
—Rod Serling, "The Twilight Zone" (CBS)

23

"Lieutenant, are you all right?" I demanded.

"Yeah, yeah," he said. "My pride hurts the most. Nobody ever surprised me with a knife like that before."

Falzet offered him a handkerchief to wrap around the hand. As he took it, he said, "Look, Mrs. Schick, put that knife away, please? You're going to hurt yourself."

She laughed at that, a girlish giggle. "How could I possibly hurt myself, Lieutenant? How could I be hurt anymore?"

He took a step toward her again, she pressed the point against her throat harder. It made a kind of obscene dimple.

"I warned you to get away!" she snapped. "Believe me, I know just where to put this. I've had practice."

"Mrs. Schick," I said respectfully.

"Yes?"

"You took that knife from Devlin, didn't you?"

"Yes. The coward. It was meant for you, you know. That fool. When he failed Wednesday night, he called me and said he'd try again tomorrow. He thought you'd take him to your apartment. I was to call to distract you. So you'd turn your back on him. I don't know why he didn't. He stabbed his friend in the back."

"Why? Why did you want to kill me?"

"Why? Don't be a hypocrite, Mr. Cobb. You've destroyed me, you don't have to gloat. You were plotting with that slut of a daughter of mine. You knew, I could tell. You knew, Carlson told you. I knew you knew when you came to the Willowdale hospital the day after the murder."

"Did you know Devlin was going to kill Carlson?"

"*Stop it!* You know I did!" Her face was twisted and distorted. *The face is the mirror of the soul,* I thought. "Devlin warned me to keep my mouth shut," she went on.

180

"But when you came to the hospital, you didn't say anything to me about the murder. *Then* I knew. You were plotting wth *her*. You were going to destroy me, so *she* would get control of Walter's stock and my stock, and add it to hers, and take over the Network."

Cynthia Schick looked at her daughter with hatred. Roxanne looked at her and cried.

"Mrs. Schick," I said softly, "I know you won't believe me, but I swear I wasn't sure you had anything to do with it until Fred Barber told me he gave you your husband's wallet on Wednesday. It was the use of your husband's license that tipped me off, and the missing page with the picture that turned up in Devlin's wallet that confirmed it.

"I never wanted to destroy you, Mrs. Schick. It was just the only way it made sense. Carlson was killed by Devlin, then Devlin was killed. A blackmailer and his victim have a common interest in seeing that a third person doesn't reveal the secret. That's what accounts for the murder of Carlson and the attacks on me.

"Then, I guess, the temptation to remove the blackmailer was irresistible. Was that how it was?"

"No," she said sharply. "I never even *thought* of killing him until Thursday afternoon, when he called me and told me to meet him at your apartment. I drove into the city.

"He was a fool. He wanted to go to Goldfarb—he had heard of him from Carlson—and tell him about ARGUS. He said with Goldfarb's backing, he could make millions—that *we* could. He planned to make me his mistress. As though I would do that to Walter!"

Of course. Devlin should have known. Just because a woman commits fraud, and connives at homicide, it doesn't mean she's ready for adultery. It was too ironic not to laugh at.

"That's right! Laugh at me! He laughed, too. That's when I knew I had to be rid of him. I took the steak knife from your kitchen. It was expensive, I knew it could be traced back to that apartment. I told Devlin I was bringing him back to my house and . . . well, I let him think what he wanted. I let him drive. When we came to a good place, I said I was carsick and made him pull over, then put the knife in his neck."

"Did you take the second switchblade from him then?"

"Yes. I . . . I don't know why. I took Walter's license back, too."

"You should have burned it."

"I know that now. I didn't want to." She started to sob. "I failed him, I always fail. Except now. Walter is free, I freed him from that machine after you called, pulled the plug—"

Roxanne Schick screamed and bolted from the office.

Lieutenant Martin pointed Falzet's bloody handkerchief at one of his men. "Check on it," he barked.

During the distraction, I had circled to my right, until I was just a couple of steps from Mr. Hewlen's desk. I reached over and picked up his telephone.

"What are you doing?" Cynthia Schick demanded.

"Don't mind me," I told her. "I don't care what you do anymore."

I dialed extension 223. I was prepared to fake it, but the phone was answered.

"Jack Hansen."

"Jack? Matt Cobb." I looked over at Cynthia Schick. She was beyond help, now; her face was a death mask. Still, she wasn't going to kill herself without everyone paying attention.

"Jack, Cynthia Schick is about to kill herself, because she can't face the consequences of two, or possibly three murders she's been in on, not to mention maybe hurting American television beyond all repair.

"So get up here right away with a minicam, a soundman, and some lights, maybe plug in on the air live, so she can have the whole prime-time audience to watch her. I'll ask her to wait until you get here."

I looked up at a noise, a cry of animal fury from Cynthia Schick, who was springing at me, switchblade raised high.

I dropped the phone, and used some Army judo on her. It was a simple move. It would have been harder if she'd come with the knife underhand, the right way. It ended with her prone on the rug with my knee in her back.

Rivetz picked up the knife, then stood over her with Lieutenant Martin. They both had their guns drawn.

I got up, carefully, but Cynthia Schick didn't move.

I picked up the phone.

"Matt?" Jack Hansen's voice said. "Matt? What the hell's going on there? Are you crazy?"

"Yes," I said wearily. "I'm a goddam lunatic. I'm sending Harris Brophy and Shirley Arnstein down with a story. Good-bye."

Lieutenant Martin gingerly turned Cynthia Schick's trembling body face up. Her lips were slack, and quivered with the vibrations of her body. Her eyes were wide and unblinking. They were focused on something far away I couldn't see.

> *"Good night and good luck."*
> —Edward R. Murrow, "See It Now" (CBS)

24

It took over two hours, until the police were out of there. I remember it only as snatches of conversation.

Like one of the three psychiatrists (one official, two unofficial) who were doing a skull survey on Mrs. Schick saying to the others, "Complete schizoid withdrawal," and the other two nodding solemnly.

And this exchange I had with Harris Brophy, when he returned from the newsroom:

"She was right after all, Matt."

"What do you mean by that?"

"You *did* destroy her. You took her big death scene and made a joke out of it. That was the crowning insult that put her away."

And this one with Horace A. Rivetz:

"Cobb, that was incredible. I apologize for everything."

I was overwhelmed. "Thanks," I said. We shook hands.

Mr. Hewlen's voice kept playing the refrain of the evening. "I loved her. I tried to be a good father to her. I tried to make it up to her. I did. I . . . " He never finished it.

At one point, Goldfarb said, "A remarkably entertaining evening, Mr. Cobb. Consider that offer for a position in my organization to be still open."

"What makes you think you still have an organization?"

He just gave me his Ozzie Nelson smile and walked away.

Lieutenant Martin was angry with me. "You held out on me, Matty. I don't like it."

"I didn't either. I was trying to protect the Network. That was my job. Unfortunately, it didn't work out."

"Yeah, unfortunately. Did it ever occur to you that if you leveled with me from the start, Devlin would still be alive and that woman wouldn't be heading to the soft room?"

"It occurred to me," I admitted. "But *you* heard her. I was out to get her, *everyone* was out to get her. She was a time bomb. I'm glad it was Devlin who was around and not her daughter, say, when she went off. I'm very glad.

"Speaking of Roxanne, have you heard anything from Willowdale?"

"Yeah, my man caught up with Roxanne outside and went up there with her. It appears that Walter Schick has double-crossed his wife and surprised all the doctors by living without the respirator. The same way Karen Quinlan did over in Jersey. Maybe we're tougher than we think, Matty."

"Maybe," I said.

Eventually, the room quieted down; the doctors and detectives were through with their various investigations, and the prisoner/patient had been taken away. The only noise was the slow chanting of Mr. Hewlen: "I tried, I tried, I . . ." Falzet was trying to comfort him.

I sat on the love seat and closed my eyes, trying to relax. No luck. My memory insisted on doing a high-speed playback of the last four days, and I was too tired to fight it.

And then the tar pit began to churn again.

The case wasn't finished quite yet.

I waited until the last policeman had left, and I was alone with Falzet and Mr. Hewlen at the top of the Tower of Babble.

"Mr. Hewlen," I said. "Mr. Falzet, we need to have a little talk."

The talk didn't take as long as I expected it to, for the simple reason that I was the only one who said anything. When I finished, I left to let what I had said sink in.

I took the elevator downstairs, waved good-bye to Wilkie the guard, took Spot out of the company car (I no longer felt I had a right to drive it), and walked through the rain to the apartment.

"I think we're going to be spending a lot more time together, Spot old boy," I told him. He licked my hand.

I unlocked the apartment door, went in, changed the water in Spot's dish, took off my jacket and tie, grabbed a big handful of Squirrel Nuts candy, and collapsed on the sofa to eat them.

I forced myself to eat three before I grabbed the phone

185

and tried to call Monica. There was no answer at her apartment. She couldn't have been visiting Tony this late.

Maybe she had tried to call me. Rick and Jane had one of those automatic answering things on their phone, but I hardly ever used it because I got so few calls.

There was a message there, all right.

"Matt Cobb," Monica's voice scolded me. "Where have you *been?* I've been trying to call you since the plane landed, and all I get is this stupid recording. Great news! I got the part, I got it! They're going to announce it at a press conference on Monday, but I'm so excited, I decided to fly out right away. I'll send my address as soon as I have one. Bye bye. My love to Spot."

Click. And that was it.

"She did it to me again!" I yelled, I guess to Spot. "I let her do it to me again!"

Another phone call after the fact, just what I needed to make the night complete. I shook my head. I would never understand that girl. She loved me with all her heart . . . when I was around and handy. I tried to hate her, but couldn't quite do it.

I was still trying when the doorbell rang. I opened the door to see Roxanne Schick, with her dark hair plastered to her head, and her clothes soaking wet from the rain.

"Can I come in, Cobb?" she asked meekly. "Please?"

I got out of her way and let her in. She didn't want to sit on anything and get the upholstery wet, so I got her a chrome and plastic chair from the kitchen. She straddled it backwards, and rested her chin on her arms folded across the back.

I told her I was glad she came.

She looked surprised. "You are? I've been walking around for hours, ever since the police finished with me, debating with myself whether or not to come up here."

"Why should you have to debate?"

"I'm a monster, Cobb, I've told you all along. I'm poison. I'm no good, the product of no-good parents. Why should you or *anybody*—?"

"Stop it!" I said. She shut up. "Look, this is stupidity, what you're saying. Your mother is a sick, scared woman. Your father . . ."

"Yes," she said in a deadly voice, "my beloved father. *He* wasn't sick, he was just greedy. That argument they had that night—that wasn't about me at all! It was just

186

over paying blackmail because somebody knew about their dirty scheme."

"Not *their* scheme, Rox," I told her.

"What?"

"Your father didn't have anything to do with it. That's the problem. I blew it."

"What are you trying to say? Do you mean my parents didn't do all those terrible things?"

"No, your mother killed Devlin all right, and she was in on the ratings fix, too, but your father wasn't."

There was a strange look on Roxanne's face, as though she were begging me not to be lying.

"Look, Rox, everything I said tonight, I believed when I said it. It wasn't until later that I realized the truth.

"Remember what your mother said, how she described the fight? She said, 'Walter was furious, just furious,' and 'he was going to have it out with Father—Mr. Hewlen—the next morning.'

"It just doesn't make sense, Rox. If you've done something wrong, and a blackmailer finds out about it and puts the squeeze on, you don't get furious, for God's sake. You don't get *outraged*. You get scared to death, is what you get.

"And *have it out* with Mr. Hewlen? Stroll into the office of the Chairman of the Board and *have it out* with him that you're being blackmailed over tampering with the ratings of a Network show, and what is he going to do to help you out? That would be tantamount to suicide. No, Rox, as far as I'm concerned, that alone makes your father innocent.

"He was outraged, because *the blackmail demand he got from Devlin was the first he heard about the plot.* Your mother dealt with Carlson, *he* naturally assumed your father was behind it all, and he passed the assumption on to Devlin."

"Well, then, you mean my mother was in it alone?" Roxanne asked.

"No, Rox. Your mother gave that away, too. Remember what she kept saying all the time she was protesting your father's innocence."

" 'Tell them, Father,' " Roxanne quoted. " 'Tell them.' *She was begging my grandfather to confess!*"

"He *knew* Walter Schick was the best man for the job," I said, "but he felt he couldn't install him as President of the Network unless there was a clear indication to the

187

stockholders that it really was the best thing for the Network.

"And your mother wanted it so bad. Your grandfather had failed your mother, or at least they both felt he had. It was a way to make it up to her."

Roxanne laughed, bitterly. "He made it up to her all right. He destroyed her, he destroyed my father, he destroyed everything, even his own Network!"

"I don't know about that," I said. "I did a lot of talking for effect tonight. I think the Network can bounce back. You can bet this won't happen again. It was only a kind of perverted miracle it happened in the first place."

"But . . . what are you going to do? You're not just going to let him get away with it?"

"Of course not. But I've already done what I can do. The rest is up to you."

She was startled. "Me?"

"Yes, you. I told your grandfather and Falzet what I've figured out. To get them thinking. But I've got no proof. There can't be any proof unless your mother talks, and that's not likely.

"So I made your grandfather a promise. I happen to own twenty-seven shares of Network common stock. I promised him that if I wasn't satisfied that things had been set right by the time of the stockholders' meeting next month, I was going to exercise my right as a stockholder and ask some very embarrassing questions from the floor. And I made sure Falzet got the point."

"You want to make him resign," she said.

"Right, take his Network away from him. It's the only punishment he would understand."

"But what if he doesn't go along?"

"Then the fight really starts, only *you* have to do it. You own a big block of stock—I think second only to the Chairman of the Board himself, with your mother and father incompetent to exercise rights of ownership—I don't know the law.

"Now, Falzet owns a big chunk, too, and when the numbness wears off, he'll realize how badly he was shafted, and will howl for blood. You team up with him, and force the old man out. If it comes to that."

"But if it wasn't for Falzet, my father would have been President long ago, and my mother would never have—"

I cut her off. "Falzet played by the rules, Rox. I don't

188

like him, but he's a good businessman, and he's reasonably honest."

Roxanne accepted it, grimly. "Okay, as long as my grandfather suffers for what he did to my father. That hypocrite. He was the worst of all."

"I don't think so," I said. "I think it was Devlin. He was motivated solely by greed. He exploited, and finally killed his friend Carlson, for money. He *used* that poor Gayle Spencer, God knows what she's in for now, and *he* drove your mother off the deep end. All for money.

"But it's a funny thing. Except for Devlin, everybody in this case was motivated by the same thing—"

Spot barked as the phone rang. Before I picked up the phone I said, "That'll be Falzet."

That's who it was. After we said hello, he said, "Cobb, I want you to know that I may have been a bit hasty in firing you . . ."

"Get to the point," I told him, "it's late."

He harrumphed. "Very well. As you know, I've been conferring with Mr. Hewlen ever since you left, and . . . well, he's come to a decision."

"Care to tell me what it is?"

"Certainly, that's why I called you. Anyway, Mr. Hewlen has given me a letter of resignation, which he wants me to present to the Board of Directors at a special session tomorrow."

"Why can't he give it to them in person?"

"Mr. Hewlen is leaving tomorrow on a cruise on his yacht. He said he plans to be gone the rest of this year, possibly longer."

"Do you know the name of that yacht. Falzet?"

"It's called *Cynthia*, I believe." What a cold fish. He might have been telling me what was on ABC that was giving us rating trouble.

"He's going to kill himself," I said. "He's going to sail that boat to the middle of the ocean and jump off."

Falzet wasn't hearing things like that. "One of Mr. Hewlen's last official acts," he went on, "was to tell me to appoint you full Vice-President in charge of Special Projects. McFeeley has written to say that he doesn't intend to return to the Network after all."

"Did you talk the old man into killing himself, Falzet?"

"Of course not! The very idea makes me nauseous."

"The correct word," I told him, "is *nauseated*."

189

"What about the offer, Cobb?"

"I'll let you know." I hung up on him.

Roxanne said, "Do you really think he's going to kill himself, Cobb?"

"Yes," I told her.

"Is that what you had in mind when you told him what you knew?"

"I thought it was a possibility. Does the idea bother you?"

It sure as hell bothered me; even though the man had calmly advised me to keep quiet about the case so his crazy daughter could have another crack at killing me, it still bothered me.

Evidently, Roxanne was tougher than I was. Instead of answering the question, she said, "You were saying something about everyone but Devlin acting for the same reason. What was it?"

"Oh, that," I said. "Love. Love. Your mother committed fraud and murder because she loved your father. Mr. Hewlen sold the Network—the Network he built with his own hands—down the river because he wanted to prove he loved your mother. Carlson gimmicked the computer because he still loved Monica"—I felt a twinge at that—"Hell, even Goldfarb started his crime because he loves his mother."

"What about you, Cobb?" Roxanne asked.

"Me?" I laughed. "I did what I did, because, God help me, I love the Network."

We were silent for a long time. Then, as though there'd never been a pause in the conversation, Roxanne said, "Who loves *me*, Cobb? When the hell do I get somebody to love *me*?"

"Rox," I said, "tell you what. You go dry off and freshen up, and Spot and I will make a big pot of hot chocolate, and when you come back, I'll see if I can't answer your question. Okay?"

"Okay, Cobb," she said, smiling.

"C.I.A., Mister Fletcher."

"Um. Would you mind spelling that?"

"Enough of your bull, Fletcher."

"Okay, guys. What's the big deal?"

"You are going to tape the most private bedroom conversations of the most important people in American journalism."

"You're crazy. What have you got on me?"

"Taxes, Mister Fletcher."

"What about 'em?"

"You haven't paid any."

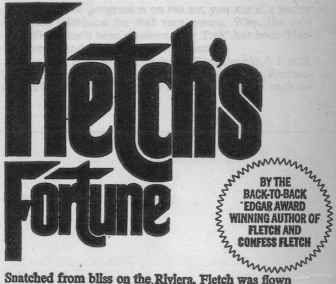

BY THE BACK-TO-BACK 'EDGAR AWARD WINNING AUTHOR OF FLETCH AND CONFESS FLETCH

Snatched from bliss on the Riviera, Fletch was flown to the journalism convention with a suitcase full of bugging devices and a bizarre assignment: dig up some juicy scandals on Walter March, the ruthless newspaper tycoon . . . Then Walter March was found lying face up with a long pair of scissors stuck in his back. It was the crime of the century. And a hell of a story.

A blockbuster of suspense by
GREGORY McDONALD

" . . . the toughest, leanest horse to hit the literary racetrack since James M. Cain."—PETE HAMILL

Avon/37978/$1.95